Marguerite Yourcenar was born Marguerite de
Crayencour in Brussels in 1903, her mother was
Belgian and her father was French. Her mother
died shortly after her birth and she was brought
up and educated by her father. She was reading
Racine and Aristophanes by the age of eight
and her father taught her Latin at ten, and
Greek at twelve. When she was eighteen he paid
for the publication of her first book of poetry
and together they worked out her pen name –
an inexact anagram of Crayencour. After her
father's death when she was twenty-four she
continued to travel throughout Europe.

Her first novel *Alexis* was published in 1929;
several essays and collections of stories
followed and by 1939 her reputation as a writer
was established. Later her great friend, the
translator Grace Frick, invited her to America.
There she lectured in comparative literature at
Sarah Lawrence College in New York, and
translated in her spare time. She also began
work again on *Memoirs of Hadrian* (she had
burned an earlier version of the manuscript)
and when the book was published in France in
1951 it was an immediate success and met with
great critical acclaim.

Marguerite Yourcenar has won several literary
honours but in 1981 she entered the ranks of
the 'Immortals' when she was elected – the first
woman ever to be so – to the Académie
Française. One of the most respected writers in
the French language, she has published many
novels, several plays, critical essays, and poetry,
as well as two volumes of memoirs. She is
currently working on a third. Her letters and
journals, including her correspondence with
Grace Frick, have been deposited with Harvard
University, where they w...
fifty years after her dea...

Also by Marguerite Yourcenar
COUP DE GRACE
and published by Black Swan

A Coin in Nine Hands

Marguerite Yourcenar

Translated from the French by
Dori Katz in collaboration with the author

BLACK SWAN

A COIN IN NINE HANDS

A BLACK SWAN BOOK 0 552 99120 1

Originally published in Great Britain by Aidan Ellis Publishing Limited

PRINTING HISTORY
Aidan Ellis edition published 1983
Black Swan edition published 1984

Translation copyright © 1982 by Farrar, Straus & Giroux, Inc.

Originally published in French, *Denier du rêve*, copyright © 1934 by Editions Bernard Grasset; revised edition copyright © 1959 by Librairie Plon; copyright © 1971 by Editions Gallimard.

This book is set in 11/12 Mallard

Black Swan Books are published by
Transworld Publishers Ltd.,
Century House, 61–63 Uxbridge Road,
Ealing, London W5 5SA

Made and printed in Great Britain by the Guernsey Press Co. Ltd., Guernsey, Channel Islands.

To abandon one's life for a dream is to know its true worth.

–MONTAIGNE, BOOK III, CHAPTER IV

A Coin in Nine Hands

A Coin in Nine Hands

Paolo Farina was a man from the provinces, still young, rather prosperous, as honest as can be expected of someone on intimate terms with the law, and popular enough in his village in Tuscany not to be scorned because of his misfortune. People felt sorry for him when his wife ran away to Libya to follow a lover she hoped would make her happy. For she had not been happy the six months she kept house for Paolo Farina and had to take the nonstop advice of a shrill mother-in-law. But Paolo, himself blindly happy to possess this young woman and separated from her by his dense satisfaction, had not been aware of her restlessness. When she left, after a scene that humiliated him in front of the two maids, he was surprised that he had been unable to make her love him.

But his neighbors' judgements reassured him; she must be guilty, he thought, since the little town commiserated with him. Angiola's flight was blamed on her southern blood; everyone knew the young woman came from Sicily. But people were appalled that she had fallen so low, seeing that she came from a good family and had had the good fortune to have been brought up in Florence at the Convent of Noble-women, and seeing, furthermore, that she had been so well received in Pietrasanta. Everyone agreed that, all in all, Paolo had been a perfect husband. More perfect than the village realized, since Paolo had met, helped, then married Angiola under circumstances in which a prudent man would ordinarily not marry. But he did not use these

11

reminders, as he could have, to blame Angiola for even more ingratitude, because he himself had already forgotten them. He had done his best to erase these details from his memory, mostly as a kindness to his young wife, to make her forget what he called her misadventure, and in part as a kindness to himself, because it is not pleasant to be reminded that the woman one possesses fell in one's arms more or less on the rebound.

When she was present, he had placidly cherished her; absent, Angiola shone with all the fires other men could evidently light in her; he missed, not the wife he lost, but the mistress she had never been to him. He did not expect to see her again: he had quickly given up the extravagant idea of taking the boat to Tripoli, where, for the time being, the opera troupe Angiola's lover belonged to was performing. Moreover, he did not even wish for her return anymore: he was only too aware that for her he would always be the ridiculous husband who complains at suppertime that the noodles are not well done. His evenings were sad in that pretentious new house, decorated by Angiola in a childish bad taste that gave each knick-knack an exaggerated importance, but a house that nevertheless bore witness to the absent woman because, fragile like her good intentions, each object showed her effort to take an interest in his life and an attempt, by dint of adorning the rooms, to disregard the mediocrity of the main actor, himself. She had tried to bind herself to the home with these pink ribbons that Paolo, randomly opening half-empty drawers, got entangled in.

He started taking business trips to Rome a little more often than was really necessary; these allowed him to visit his sister-in-law to find out if by chance she had any news of Angiola. But the attraction of the capital was also in part a reason for those trips, as was the opportunity for certain pleasures a man of his position would not have dared in Florence, pleasures that were not available in Pietrasanta. Suddenly he was dressing with a more showy vulgarity, imitating, without realizing it,

12

the man Angiola had chosen over him. He started to take an interest in the indolent, talkative girls crowding the cafés and streets of Rome. Some had behind them, like Angiola, the memory of a household, a seducer, a desertion, or at least so he thought. One afternoon in a park, he met Lina Chiari near a fountain babbling the same words of coolness over and over again. She was neither prettier nor younger than the others: he was still shy: she was daring; she spared him the first words and almost the first moves. He was stingy; she was not demanding, precisely because she was poor. What's more, like Angiola, she had been brought up in a convent in Florence, although it wasn't exactly an institution for noblewomen. She knew all the local news, knew about the construction of a bridge, about the fire at a school, all these small things that allow people of the same town to share common landmarks of the past. He found again in her voice the throaty sweetness of Florentine women. And since all women have more or less the same body, and possibly the same soul, when Lina was speaking and the light had been turned off, he forgot that Lina was not Angiola and that his Angiola had not loved him.

Love can't be bought. Women who sell themselves to men, after all, only rent themselves out; but dreams can be bought; these intangible goods are sold in many forms. The little money Paolo Farina gave Lina each week was used to create for him a welcome illusion; that is to say, perhaps the only thing in the world that does not deceive.

Feeling tired, Lina Chiari leaned against a wall and ran her hand across her forehead. She lived far from the center of town; the bumpy bus ride had been painful; she was sorry she didn't take a taxi. But that day she had promised herself to be economical; even though the first week of the month had gone by, she hadn't paid her landlady yet; she still wore, in spite of the heat of this April day in Rome, a winter coat with a scraggy fur collar. She owed money to the pharmacist for the last batch of pills she had bought: those had been useless; she was unable to sleep.

It was not yet three o'clock; she strolled on the shady side of the Corso. Shops were beginning to reopen. Still groggy from lunch and the siesta, a few people leisurely walked by on their way back to the office or the shops. Lina did not attract their attention: she walked fast. The success of streetwalking is in proportion to the slowness of a woman's ambling and to the quantity of her makeup, for, of all the promises of a face or a body, the only one that is completely convincing is that of availability. Lina had considered it more proper not to wear makeup to go to the doctor's office. Besides, finding herself looking worse than usual, she preferred to be able to tell herself it was because she wasn't wearing any rouge.

After hesitating for many months, trying to deny her illness, she was keeping her appointment reluctantly. She had told no one; as long as it was hidden, her illness seemed less serious. The alarm signal of terror had awakened her too late, in the middle of the night, her

14

body already beleaguered by the enemy, only just in time to prevent escape. Like the inhabitants of besieged medieval cities who, surprised by death, went back to bed, trying to fall asleep again by telling themselves that the threatening flames were only a nightmare, Lina had used the drugs that put oblivion between us and terror; these benefactors too often called upon had grown weary of helping her. Shyly, with her casual encounters she had begun jokingly to allude to her insomnia, to her very obvious weight loss, which delighted her, she said, since it made her look like those fashionable French magazine models. Although she tossed off her illness as a slight fatigue so that each of her clients could easily ignore it, still she was hurt by their lack of interest, by their not noticing that she was lying.

As for her lump, Lina herself could easily find and feel it, but it was almost invisible; at most, it looked like a small swelling hidden beneath the folds of a tired breast; this, Lina did not talk about, fearing that one of her clients might discover it by chance in a caress; she insisted as much as possible on keeping on her slip, becoming modest again now that her flesh might harbor a mortal danger. But her silence grew heavier, hardened, as though it, too, were a malignant tumor slowly poisoning her. At last she had decided to see a doctor, not so much for a cure as to be able to talk about herself openly. Her friend Massimo, the only person she half confided in, who knew everybody in Rome, at least by name, suggested she consult Dr. Sarte; he could even, thanks to someone he knew, get her an appointment with this new medical celebrity. A week ago, Lina Chiari had called his office from a public phone in a bar; she had carefully written down the address and the hour of her appointment on a piece of paper that thereupon became like a talisman or the medal of a saint in her purse. And brave because she was defeated, hoping for nothing but not to have to give up hope too quickly, she was nevertheless happy to be in the hands of a wellknown doctor and appeared at the appointed time at the door of

Professor Alessandro Sarte, specialist in internal diseases, former director of a surgical clinic, whose office hours were three to six, Tuesdays, Thursdays, and Fridays (closed during summer months).

Disregarding the elevator, out of humility (besides, she never quite trusted these machines), she started up the white marble staircase. It was almost cold here, which immediately seemed to vindicate the wearing of her old winter coat. She found the plaque bearing the name on the second floor. She rang the bell timidly, awed by the solemn, old-fashioned house, which reminded her of the palace of a benevolent great lady in Florence that she was sent to every year with a bouquet of flowers and birthday wishes. A nurse opened the door; she looked like the private nurse of the old Florentine lady; she too was dressed in a smock and had a professional kindness about her. There were people in the beautiful waiting room, whose venetian blinds protected the wallpaper from the sun. An older man went first; he stared at Lina and she couldn't help but smile back; then it was an old woman's turn. Nothing could be said about her except that she was very old; a woman and a child went in next. As soon as these people passed the door that then closed on them, they might as well be dead, since they did not come back; noticing that some of them were as poorly dressed as herself, Lina stopped worrying about the doctor's fee. She was angry at herself, however, for not having consulted, as she had first planned, the general practitioner who had treated her for something having to do with her love life. Like the village folks from around Florence, she had changed saints at the moment of danger.

Dr. Alessandro was sitting behind a desk littered with files; only his head, his chest, his hands resting like carefully polished instruments on the table, could be seen. His handsome, slightly grimacing face reminded Lina of the dozens of other kinds of faces one noticed on the street, faces that even in the most intimate moments remained anonymous, faces of men passing whom she would not see again. But Dr. Sarte consorted only with a higher rank of women in the aristocracy of hired flesh. Lina, explaining her symptoms, started to play down the seriousness of her apprehensions, stretching her story with useless information like a patient taking forever to uncover his wound, describing her visit as simply a precaution, perhaps unnecessary; her light tone had in it a certain amount of courage and the secret wish that the doctor would not contradict her. Then, like a man who has had enough of the chitchat of a casual mistress and is in a hurry to get to the naked truth, Dr. Sarte said: 'Get undressed.'

There is no evidence that Lina recognized those familiar words coming from a doctor and not from a client. While her hands struggled with the snaps of her clothing, Dr. Sarte felt obliged to add words straight out of his kit of medical formulas; they were words Lina hadn't heard since the very distant past of her first seduction: 'Don't worry, I won't hurt you.'

He made her go into a room that felt cold because of a huge window, whose light seemed likewise pitiless. She didn't even have to fake a shudder when those big clean hands felt her body for no voluptuous purpose. Blinking as she lay on a leather couch hardly bigger than her own body, she tried to read the doctor's pupils—they seemed monstrously big for being so close, but his gaze revealed nothing. Besides, the word she dreaded was not uttered; the surgeon only reproached her for not coming to him sooner. Suddenly calm, she felt as though she had nothing more to fear, since, of all her terrors, the very worst had already happened.

Standing behind the screen where the doctor had left her so she could get dressed, she lifted the ribbon of her silk shirt and stopped a moment to look at her breasts as she used to do when, as an adolescent, she had marveled at the slow maturation of her body. But today a much more terrible ripening was taking place. A distant episode came back to her: summer camp; Bocca d'Arno Beach; she was swimming by some rocks when an

17

octopus fastened on her flesh. She screamed, she tried to run, weighed down by this hideous living burden. They had been able to remove the animal only by tearing it off her body. All her life, she had kept the memory of those insatiable tentacles, of her blood and of the scream which had scared even herself but which would be useless now since this time no one could free her. While the doctor called to make arrangements at the hospital for her, tears that flowed from the very depths of her childhood started to stream down her gray trembling face.

Toward four-thirty, the doctor's door opened again and the nurse put Lina Chiari in the elevator. The doctor had been all kindness to her; he gave her some of the port he kept on hand, in his cabinet, for these occasions when patients lose heart. He was taking care of everything; all she had to do was show up next week at the hospital where he operated on the poor for free; to hear him, nothing was easier than getting better, or dying. The elevator ended its vertical three-story dive; Lina remained seated on the red velvet bench, her head in her hands. Still, while sunk in grief, she savored the consolation of telling herself that she would no longer have to worry about finding money, about cooking or doing her laundry, that, from now on, all she had to do was suffer.

Once again, she was on the Corso, now full of noise and dust; newspaper venders were yelling about a sensational crime. A hackney carriage standing by the curb reminded her of her father; he was a coachman; he had two horses; one was called Bello, the other Buono; her mother took care of them more tenderly than she had her children. Buono fell ill; he had to be done away with. Lina walked by without noticing a poster announcing a speech by the Chief of State for this very evening, but stopped, out of habit, by an ad for the movie theater Mondo, where this week a great adventure film featuring the incomparable Angiola Fides was playing. In front of a linen store, she reminded herself that she would have to buy some decent nightgowns for the hospital, the kind

she used to wear at school; it wouldn't do to be buried in
pink silk. She felt like going home to tell her landlady
everything; but on learning she was ill, that woman
would promptly ask her to pay what she owed. Paolo
Farina would come on Monday at his usual time; no
point putting him off by telling him of her illness. The
idea occurred to her to go to a café to call Massimo, her
dearest friend; but he had never liked being disturbed;
Massimo's life was even more complicated than her
own; he only came to Lina during bad times, to be
cheered up. They couldn't change roles: tender compassion was the only thing Massimo expected of women.
She tried telling herself that it was better that way, that
it would have been harder for her to die had Massimo
loved her. She felt a compassion sharp as a flaring-up of
pain for this Lina no one pitied, who had only six more
days to live. Even if she survived the operation, she only
had six more days to live. The doctor had just told her
one of her breasts would have to be removed; mutilated
chests were appealing only on the marble statues
tourists go to see in the Vatican Museum.

Crossing a street, she noticed in the window of a cosmetics shop a woman walking toward her at that same
moment. The woman was no longer young, with big,
tired, sad-looking eyes in a drawn face that didn't try to
smile seductively. A woman so ordinary, so like a hundred other women in the throng of evening strollers, that
Lina would have walked by her without a second glance.
Yet she recognized herself in those worn clothes that,
like her own body, she had a sort of organic knowledge
of; she was as sensitive to the slightest tear, the smallest
stain on them as a sick person was to dangerous skin
blemishes. Those were her own shoes deformed by
walking, her coat bought on sale in a fashionable store,
her little, brand-new hat, loud and elegant, which
Massimo had insisted on giving her in one of those somewhat alarming moments of sudden wealth when he liked
to shower her with gifts. But she didn't recognize her
face. What she saw was not the face of the Lina Chiari

who already belonged to the past but the future face of a Lina sadly stripped of everything, a Lina who had entered those meticulously clean and sterilized zones, those zones impregnated with formaldehyde and chloroform which are the cold borders of death. A half-professional gesture made her open her purse to look for her lipstick; she found only a handkerchief, a key, a compact decorated with a four-leaf clover, a few wrinkled bills, and a new ten-lira silver piece Paolo Farina had given her the day before, hoping that the novelty of the coin would compensate for the mediocrity of the gift. She realized that she had forgotten her lipstick in the doctor's waiting room; going back to look for it was out of the question. But a lipstick was something she couldn't do without and therefore had to buy. She went into the cosmetics shop, and the owner, Giulio Lovisi, hurried to wait on her.

She came back out equipped with a lipstick and a free makeup sample from a French manufacturer. She had taken them unwrapped; fogging up with her breath the shop window that mirrored the whole life of a Roman evening parading behind her, she made up her face. Her pale cheeks became pink again; her mouth took on that rosiness that evokes the secret flesh and the flower of a healthy bosom. Her teeth, brightened by contrast, gleamed softly against her lips. The lively, passionate Lina now swept away the ghosts of the Lina to come. She would arrange to see Massimo this very evening. Deceived by the false freshness makeup had just given her, this dreaming, selfish, but tender young man, who would grow depressed at the slightest reference to physical pain, would not notice that she was stricken. Once again he would sit across from her, placing his cigarettes and his books on the coffee table; as usual, he would complain about life, and especially about himself. She would calm down by trying to cheer him up. And it might be that she could still pull it off. Some man would invite her to one of those quasi-elegant restaurants she was saving her most showy dresses for; in the evening, from a distance, and by lamplight, her girlfriends would not notice that she had changed, would not have the pleasure of feeling sorry for her. Even the dense Paolo Farina suddenly seemed less cumbersome than usual, as if his dour good health (in the eyes of this stricken woman) bestowed a kind of reassuring prestige on him. Everything seemed less gloomy to her now that her face no longer frightened her. This dazzling mask, which she herself had just created, blocked her view of the pit into which she had felt herself sliding a few moments ago. Those six days beyond which she preferred not to look promised enough happiness to make the oncoming disaster less certain; and besides, by contrast, it placed a new value on her wretched life.

A smile, as artificial as a last touch of makeup, lit up her face. Then, as forced as that smile had been, little by little it became sincere: Lina smiled to see herself smile. It didn't matter that the rouge, hurriedly applied, caked pale cheeks, that these very cheeks were only a veil of flesh on the bony frame, and that this frame was as perishable as a woman's first bloom; it didn't matter that, in turn, the skeleton would crumble into dust, leaving behind it the nothingness the human soul too often is. Party to an illusion that saved her from horror, Lina Chiari was kept from despair by a thin layer of makeup.

Locking up the drawer of his cash register, Giulio Lovisi threw a last glance at his darkened shop, where here and there a few flasks caught a touch of sunlight; he unfastened the door handle and pulled the iron gate across his store window. Even though the evening dust was harmful to his asthma, he leaned against the wall for a few moments to take in the twilight.

Giulio Lovisi had been on the Corso for thirty years now, selling perfumes, creams, and toiletries. During these thirty years, many things in the world and in Rome had had time to change. The few automobiles, which made his fragile merchandise rattle on the shelves, had multiplied in the suddenly too narrow street; shop displays, once unpretentiously framed by painted panels, were now inset between marble plaques that made one think of Campo Santo tombstones; perfumes, more and more costly, ended up being worth their liquid weight in gold; the perfume bottles themselves became stranger, more bizarre, or starker; and Giulio had aged. Wearing big hats that looked like halos or small ones that looked like helmets, women in long, then short skirts had leaned against his counter. When he was young, they had attracted him with their giggles, with their pale fingers against the velvet of powder puffs in the open drawers, and with the poses they seemed casually to take in front of all mirrors, in front of all eyes—poses always aimed at love, like the stage gestures actresses endlessly rehearse. Older now, more experienced, he would weigh with a glance their small, light souls: he ferreted

22

out the arrogant ones who used makeup as one more form of defiance; the ones in love who used it to keep from losing someone; the shy or plain ones who used ointments to hide their faces; and those, like the customer who had just bought a lipstick, for whom pleasure was only a job, demanding as all jobs are. And during those thirty years, obsequious supplier of feminine beauty, he managed to save enough money to build a villa by the sea in Ostia and he had remained faithful to his wife, Giuseppa.

Giulio closed up earlier than usual that evening; he was going to run some household errands downtown. Absentmindedly greeting his neighbor, the hat-shop owner, who was watching the street through his store window, he started walking, head down, absorbed in a sadness so commonplace that maybe no one would have been moved by it. Giulio kept telling himself that his lot was enviable and that his wife was a good woman, but there was no denying that business was down and that Giuseppa made him suffer. He had done his best to make her happy: he had tolerated hordes of brothers-in-law and sisters-in-law who came to him dragging behind them their ailments and their children; he had worked himself to the bone for these people whom she now berated him for helping. He couldn't help it if her pregnancy had been difficult, if it hadn't stopped raining in Paris on their honeymoon. He had served in the army for four years during the war, and that hadn't been a bed of roses. During that time Giuseppa, who kept the shop, met an assistant director at a bank, who she said, courted her and who naturally was vastly superior to Giulio, seeing that he had been decorated and owned a car; it wasn't his fault that she drove him away, because she was, after all, a decent woman. Giulio belonged to the law-and-order party; he patiently bore the disadvantages of a regime that guaranteed safety in the streets, in the same way that every year, without protest, he paid the insurance for his shop window. He wasn't the one who had wanted their daughter Giovanna

23

to marry this Carlo Stevo who had just been deported to an island by the special tribunal for subversive propaganda. The restrictions of the new code, the higher and higher import duties on French products, his wife's stupid scenes, the semi-widowhood of Vanna, and the unfair lot of his sweet granddaughter, who had infantile paralysis—all this conspired to make Giulio not quite the most unhappy of mortals, for there was vanity in claiming that title, but at least a poor man with his share of troubles like everyone else.

No, Giulio was in no hurry to go home to Ostia, where at night, through the thin walls, their lonely Vanna could be heard sobbing. Only her worry about the little girl kept Vanna from going over the edge; Giulio almost felt he should thank heaven for having granted her that sorrow, since it distracted her from the others. Indeed, that evening the dictator's speech gave him a good excuse to linger in town, but besides the fact that having to stand pressed in the crowd to listen to long-winded eloquence is tiring, it wasn't exactly an unmitigated pleasure to hear thundering denunciations against the enemies of the regime when one is oneself unwittingly identified with suspects and prisoners. Using this as an excuse to indulge in an ice cream or a quiet evening in a Roman café did not even occur to this homebody, this parsimonious old man. Better to go straight home to the tiny villa that seemed crammed by Giuseppa's big frame and the noise of her sewing machine, and hear her say once again that this black thread was worthless and that the exchanged buttons were still too expensive. Giuseppa's disposition soured a little more every day; it was difficult for this corpulent old woman suffering from rheumatism to have to, will-nilly, take care of the demanding little Mimi, keep house, and try to distract their poor Giovanna.

He had counted on time to improve his wife's temper. On the contrary, as Giuseppa aged, her short-comings grew as monstrous as her arms and waist. Reassured by thirty years of conjugal intimacy, she didn't try to hide them any more than she did her physical imperfections; he had to accept the fact that Giuseppa was jealous, the same way he had to accept that her hands would always be clammy. He was turning sixty; his oily face glistened as though over the years it had soaked up the oils and pomades he sold. She didn't see him as he really was; she had pieced together, in order to complain, a Giulio seducer-of-women who interested her more than the real Giulio. The day before, she had come to make a scene in the narrow shop, where the least sudden gesture threatened so many perfumes; she had forced him to fire his new salesgirl, an interesting young Englishwoman whom he had hired out of sheer charity to help him during rush hours. Miss Jones was momentarily without funds in Rome; she couldn't make it on the few conversation lessons she gave. Giulio sighed, mortified by his wife's suspicions, forgetting that he had looked a lot at Miss Jones's slim, long legs. Unlike the official calamities discussed every night at the dinner table, the departure of his touching English girl affected him alone; it was his very own little romantic sorrow.

Reverently pushing a door upholstered in soft leather worn and soiled by the repeated touch of many hands, Giulio Lovisi entered a small neighborhood church. Whereas other men went to cafés or spent their time in bars, he came here each evening to savor a feeble drop of God's liqueur. Even in religious matters, this respectable middle-class man was satisfied with only a few sips. God, whose will accounted for Giulio's miseries and for his lack of courage, seemed to reside among the golden altars so that an endless number of luckless people could come here to complain about their misfortunes and be comforted. Welcoming everyone, God would make you feel at home here. The celestial host did not stand on ceremony. You could either remain standing or flop on a seat with your packages; or you could stroll around absentmindedly, looking at a darkened painting that must be by a famous artist since, from time to time,

25

strangers would tip the custodian to show them where it was; or you could kneel to pray. Even Giulio, a man insignificant down to his problems, could deceive God by exaggerating his own anguish or flatter Him crudely by entrusting himself to His kindness. The invisible listener did not bother calling him on his lies; the marble Mary Magdalene propped against a pillar did not take offense when this fat man dressed in a beige suit managed to brush yearningly against her naked foot every time he went by. The priest, the organist, the red-uniformed sexton, the beggar under the porch of Santa Maria Minore, all took this frequent evening guest seriously. This was probably the only place in the world Giuseppa would have hesitated to make a scene in.

Rosalia di Credo, the candle vender, rose soundlessly from behind her stall and slipped toward Giulio along the rows of seats, and with the discreet whisper that is obligatory in sick rooms, in theaters, and in the house of God, asked: 'Mr. Lovisi, how is the dear little girl?'

'A little better,' whispered Giulio without conviction. 'But the new doctor says the same thing: it will take a lot of time and endless treatment. It's especially hard on her poor mother.'

On the contrary, Giulio had just been thinking that it did Vanna good to have the child to keep her busy. That's what he thought, but you need more firmness than the old man had to say what you think. In truth, the invalid didn't seem worse or better than usual. Giulio even doubted that she would ever be completely cured. But to admit that would have shown a lack of concern for this charitable old maid, would have complicated the kind of discreet but short courtesies that polite people exchange.

'Poor angel,' prompted Rosalia di Credo.

'Patience,' said Giulio humbly, 'patience.'

Rosalia lowered her voice even more, not for the sake of appearances as she had done a little while ago, but as if it were really important that they not be overheard. 'What an awful thing for your daughter that he didn't leave in time for Lausanne.'

'The idiot,' said Giulio, repressing a blasphemy that would only have proved his friendly intimacy with God. 'I always thought this Carlo would come to a bad end . . . I told him so many times . . .'

In fact, he had had no opportunity to tell Vanna's husband anything, for Carlo had quickly stopped seeing his father-in-law. But it wasn't out of vanity that Giulio wanted to appear to have lectured this famous luckless man, but out of fear; he wanted to eliminate any suspicion people might have that he had ever approved of him. Because a criminal can only be dangerous, it seemed appropriate to add, retrospectively, a portion of horror to the memories concerning Carlo—and Carlo Stevo was undoubtedly a criminal, since he was condemned.

'I always hated him,' he said.

It wasn't true. At first, he had bestowed on Carlo the feeling we have in greatest abundance, since that is how we regard some two billion human beings: indifference. Then, some ten years ago (how time flies!), when Giuseppa had rented Carlo by mail a furnished room in their villa in Ostia, Giulio had bought this difficult writer's books, taking pleasure in exaggerating for neighbors and acquaintances the fame of his tenant and the price he paid for his room. When, thin suitcase in hand, Carlo Stevo appeared on their threshold, Giulio had had difficulty connecting all those masterpieces and all that fame with the sickly, slightly stooped body of the thirty-year-old man; he seemed both too young for his reputation and prematurely old for his age; the Lovisis accorded their guest a condescending regard mixed with pity; that is to say, contempt. This pity, this contempt had reached its peak during a bout of pneumonia that almost killed Carlo Stevo; a certain familiarity had crept into their relationship with their tenant; this man of genius consumed by who knew what fire was suddenly only someone who was sick, whom they tried their best to nurse. But another soul caught fire: Vanna's. Such was the power of expansion of this young woman's love that the Lovisis ended up seeing Carlo through her eyes and loving him through her heart. When he became their son-in-law, what they felt was pride, for at that moment they thought of him as something they owned. They had resigned themselves to seeing their daughter only rarely: they boasted of the brand-new apartment their Vanna had in Rome in the newly developed Parioli neighborhood, and of the huge sums of money spent on the sick child. Then, when unsettling gossip began to circulate about Carlo Stevo's political associations, when their Vanna—neglected, she said, and in any case unhappy— came back to stay with them for longer and longer periods of time, finally taking refuge with them with her invalid daughter, they shook their heads, saying that, after all, it was a mistake to marry above your class, that one had good reason to mistrust a man of letters, who did not think like everyone else. And now that he was only a five-digit number on a rocky island somewhere, this unreal Carlo haunted them like a ghost.

'And,' asked Rosalia di Credo, 'did they tell you where he is?'

'Yes,' said Giulio. 'On an island. I really don't know where. Near Sicily.'

'Sicily . . .' repeated Rosalia di Credo softly.

You could tell that Sicily had awakened in her emotions more intimate but more painful perhaps than those evoked by the slight concern for another person's misfortune. The poignant echo of a lost joy had suddenly slipped in among these insipid feelings of polite interest and vague pity. If Giulio hadn't been deafened by the din of his own troubles, this simple utterance would have shown him in Rosalia a woman exiled from happiness.

'It wouldn't be so bad,' he added, 'if our poor Vanna were a little bit more reasonable. My wife has to get up every night to pray with her, coax her to drink warm milk, tuck her into bed, what have you, to try to calm her. All this because his lordship dabbled in politics and is now being bored to death on a rock. And to think that it is always the innocent who have to suffer. Impossible to sleep now.'

28

The innocent was of course himself, Giulio, whose sleep was being disturbed. The fear of insomnia made him grimace—his face now like the classical mask of a slave linked by a twist of fate to Prometheus' destiny.

'To have the nerve to attack our great statesman,' he went on, in a low voice but in the tone taken by those who know they are expressing honorable, approved feelings that no one would dare contradict. 'And a man who is successful in whatever he does. When I think that we gave our Vanna to someone we thought educated . . .'

Rosalia di Credo sighed, and this sigh was undoubtedly for her own worries. 'Holy Virgin!'

And motivated by self-interest and also by the pious sentiments of a time of her life long past, sentiments that still made her gesticulate like a little puppet over her display of candles, she said: 'Mr. Lovisi, if you lit a candle, the Madonna would help you perhaps: she is so kind.'

'The Holy Mother!' whispered Giulio.

And he stopped talking, unaware that with those words he had linked Mary to the ancient Benevolent Goddesses men still pray to. And indeed, the organ had just released above their heads its hoarse cry, too unexpected to clearly mark the beginning of a hymn. A second chord explained the first; then followed a series of pertinent questions and precise answers that nobody (except perhaps the blind organist up there) understood but that everyone thought beautiful; transformed by the pipes and bellows into sonorous waves, a pure mathematical world was taking shape; the prelude drowned out even the muted din of Rome's buses and taxis that one, however, no longer noticed, out of habit. The benediction went on in a side chapel, absentmindedly attended by a stranger drawn there by the fame of a Caravaggio fresco, and by a few women. Giulio Lovisi would not have recognized among them a person in a traveling suit who was none other than his charming English girl. A dozen faithful, ever out-distanced by the priest's clear delivery, took up in chorus the appellations of the litany, not even trying to make sense of them, too busy accomplishing a sort of continuous vocal genuflection. Those who, on the contrary, were not praying were listening, allowing from time to time a certain combination of words, one of those random epithets heard only in church, to sound something in them, confirm a thought, prolong or stir an echo from the past.

'House of Gold.'

Rosalia di Credo was unwittingly thinking of a house in Sicily.

'Queen of Martyrs.'

A young woman who had come in for shelter from a sudden rain shower raised her black shawl around her neck, smoothed its folds, and gathered it across her bosom, hiding under it the dangerous object wrapped in brown paper that perhaps tonight would change the destiny of a people.

... Let's hope the dampness ... In any case, she thought, I don't have to worry about the gun merchant, he's a member of the party. Sometimes one succeeds in these things ... More often than one would think if you are really determined to go all the way, to burn all bridges behind you. Luckily, I learned to shoot with Alessandro at Reggiomonte ... The balcony or the door? Facing the balcony, in the crowd, it will be harder to move, to raise your arm. But the door is more closely watched ... It's better to have an alternative ... you'll decide on the spot ... In the long run, it would have been wiser to choose the Villa Borghese ... Manage to stand by the bridal path, a child in hand ... No, no, don't waver ... Soon I'll be dead; that is the only sure thing. What are they saying? Queen of Heaven ... Regina Coeli: that's the name of a prison ... Perhaps in it tomorrow, I'll ... Dear God, see to it that I die right away. See to it that my death is not useless. See to it that my hand is steady, see to it that he dies ... Well, how funny. I was praying without realizing it.

'Ivory Tower ...'

Clement Roux, the old painter, let his swollen hands, the hands of a man with heart trouble, hang between his knees, bent his head to follow the spiral of words slowly sinking in his mind, until they landed on a fixed memory. Golden, smooth, naked . . . the little girl on the beach one night, could it be twenty years ago? Ivory Tower . . . Is there an expression in the world that better evokes the architecture of a young body?

'Mystical Rose . . . Chosen Vessel . . .'

Giulio has just realized that he has forgotten to pick up Mimi's medication at the pharmacy on the Corso. He is not listening. But the chosen vessel, in any case, is for him only a consecrated term with no connection with his expensive flasks and their seductive names. For, in his own time, rose water had been replaced by synthetic perfumes.

'Health of Invalids . . .'

That's true: sometimes she cures people. Especially at Lourdes. But Lourdes is far and the trip is expensive. And she didn't cure Mimi, even though everyone prayed and prayed. Maybe we didn't pray enough . . .

'Consolation of the Afflicted . . . Queen of Virgins . . .'

Miss Jones, having come back to Santa Maria Minore to hear a little music before her departure, lowers her head: she has recognized Giulio Lovisi and prefers that he not see her. She shudders, remembering the scene that the wife of this somewhat common though perfectly respectable merchant made, so vulgar. Just because she agreed to work a few days for the smallest of salaries (she lacks a work permit), while waiting for the modest allowance her accountant sends her. This trip to Italy had been madness: she had been wrong to accept the au-pair position offered by an enthusiastic fellow countryman striving in vain to make a go of a pension for British tourists in a picturesque corner of Sicily. And she should not have allowed them to fire her without at least being reimbursed for expenses. The few pounds she has just received from England barely cover her return trip. Today, however, she had allowed herself a

31

few pleasures: she had had lunch in an English tearoom on Piazza di Spagna; she had taken a guided tour of St. Peter's Dome; she had bought a holy medal for her friend Gladys, who is Irish; she was going to spend the evening at the movies before her train left. In a spirit of imitation, she joined hands mechanically, both embarrassed and seduced by these rituals of a foreign religion. She invokes the Lord to ask to have her secretary's job back in London. No matter where you are, it never hurts to pray.

Orapronobis . . . Orapronobis . . . Orapronobis . . .

Pray for us. Those three Latin words, soldered into one another, no longer belonged to any language, depended on no grammar. They were only an incantation muttered through clenched lips, a complaint, a hazy call to a vague someone. The opium of the poor, thinks Marcella scornfully. Carlo was right. They are taught that all power comes from above. None of these people would be capable of saying no.

How beautiful, thought Miss Jones, whose eyes cloud with tears—both sentimental and pure. What a pity that I'm not Catholic . . .

We didn't pray enough . . . Leaning over the tray of labeled candles, Giulio Lovisi chose five, not too thin, which would have shown stinginess, but not too thick, which would have been ostentatious. Five candles. Rosalia di Credo's gentle eyes berated him sweetly for spoiling the Madonna. I need one for Mimi, he thought; one for Vanna; one for Carlo; one especially to ask heaven that Giuseppa make life easier. And (though not putting her on the same level as the rest of the family) one for the likable Miss Jones.

For Giulio, living in a world of uncomplicated ideas, a votive candle was only a nobler, finer taper of wax, a good thing to offer the Virgin when you have a favor to ask; a thing that burns and melts on the altar on a metal

32

stem, and the sexton doesn't forget to blow it out when it's time to close the church. But the wax object, paraffin disguised as wax, lived a mysterious life. Well before Giulio, men had appropriated the labor of bees to offer the results to the gods; century after century, they had surrounded their holy relics with an honor guard of tiny flames, as they projected on their gods their own instinctive fear of the dark. Giulio's ancestors had needed rest, health, money, love: these unknown people had offered candles to the Virgin Mary in the same way that their ancestors, buried even deeper in the accumulations of time, had offered honey cakes to Venus' hot mouth. These flickerings had been consumed infinitely faster than brief human lives: some wishes had been denied; others, on the contrary, granted: the unfortunate thing is that, because wishes sometimes come true, the agony of hoping is perpetuated. Then, without asking for it, these people had obtained the only salvation that's certain, the dark gift that obliterates all others. But Giulio Lovisi was not thinking of the dead. Kneeling, he clasped his thick hands; they seemed to take their joining position as just one more pose. He felt himself yielding to the euphoria of having missed his train. Since he was late anyhow, Giuseppa's greeting could not be any worse if he came home one hour later still. And, as if taking refuge in a corner of his childhood, the tired old man stammered an *Ave* so that everything would get better.

He knew (or should have known) that nothing would get better, that things would follow their certain and irreversible decline, that the feelings and circumstances constituting his life would continue to disintegrate daily like objects that have been over-used. Giuseppa's disposition would get worse with age and rheumatism: even the Madonna couldn't change the temperament of a sixty-year-old woman. Vanna would go on leading this solitary life she was not made for, and that would lead her to desperate temptations. Perhaps she would take a lover; then she would suffer even more than up to now, because shame would be added to her

33

troubles. As it happens with many people, Giovanna's body was not suited to her soul: one or the other would have had to be different for her not to suffer. Even if she was faithful to Carlo, whom she had loved, the man who came back (if he did come back) would bear less resemblance than ever to the Carlo Stevo of her love. In his heart, Giulio also knew that their Vanna, embittered by her disappointments, was no longer the beautiful, romantic girl the famous man had fallen for: far from it. In fact, it was not even wise to wish for the return of this incautious son-in-law, ulcerated by now by misfortune and rancor, who would always be suspect to the authorities. And Mimi too (though he should not even think it) bore no resemblance to the angelic invalid he liked to picture smiling on white pillows. Even cured, the child would probably always be too delicate to marry: Giulio felt sorry for her, as though he himself had been blessed with boundless felicity, as if their Vanna had not had her share of trouble.

He would never see Miss Jones again: she would return to her rainy country, taking with her the image of a too-kind man who had been unable to silence the ill-tempered Giuseppa. For her to be once more by his side in the little shop on the Corso, and for him to treat her as he scarcely dared to in his dreams, he would have had to be rich, to be free, to be daring, and for her to be so badly stranded that she would allow herself to be loved. To picture himself free, he had to imagine committing as many crimes as a renowned murderer. Without money worries, family problems, and the weakness that made him accept them, Giulio Lovisi would have been a different man; such a transformation would have meant a more absolute death than the one that awaited him. For his death, or his wife's death—being perhaps prepared at this very moment by a thousand tiny physical occurrences—was woven into the banal pattern of small miseries that made up their lives: he could predict, were he the first to die, how Giuseppa would tell the neighbors, and how many people would bother to come to the cemetery. He had gradually become incapable of anything but this hateful, easy routine that at least relieved him of all effort. Even happiness, had happiness been possible, would have changed nothing in the poverty of his lot, for this poverty emanated from his soul. Had he been clairvoyant, Giulio Lovisi would have agreed that praying was futile. And yet the thin wax tapers burning under the unmoving gaze of the Madonna were not useless: they were there to maintain the fiction of a hope.

If anyone had asked Rosalia di Credo's neighbors about her, the general opinion would have been that she was a plain, stingy old maid who had nursed her infirm mother with affection but sent her father off to the poorhouse without a word and quarreled with her sister Angiola, who had been clever enough to find a husband. They would add that she lived on such and such a street, at such and such a number at such and such a building. All this would have been false: Rosalia di Credo was beautiful, beautiful with the slim good looks that need only the slightest bit of fleshing out to be evident. Weariness, and not time, had brought to her features the kind of erosion that humanizes even church statues; she was stingy like all who have just enough money for a single expense and enough fire for a single passion. She despised, not her sister, but her sister's husband, who had taken her sister from her; her father, not her mother, had been the love of her childhood; and she lived in Gemara.

A lot of people would have described Gemara as an old house in Sicily. This would have been a gross, altogether misleading oversimplification; every single house has something particular about itself, especially when successive owners, by adding and removing, have turned it into a stone enigma. Indeed, the estate that a Ruggero di Credo had received as fief about six centuries before had not been spared by time—that exterior time which ignores man but looms in the passage of the seasons, in the collapse of an overhanging ledge nudged to the ground by its precarious position, in

36

the slow, concentric thickening of oak trunks, those oaks that give us a sense of vegetable time measured by sap flow. Time had treated those walls and beams the same way it had treated rocks and branches; it had added its destructive commentaries to the naively obvious meanings of this human endeavor. But to say simply that it had ravaged Gemara was to forget that Time, like Janus, is a two-faced god. Evaluated in terms of generations, and littered with the downfall of regimes and the disintegration of families, human time was the true cause of these incoherent changes and these aborted projects that make up what is called, from a distance, the stability of the past. The woods, once listed in royal grants as well stocked with wild game, had been devastated by the human passion to kill animals and to cut down trees, so that the ruins of a hunting pavilion dating back to the time of the Hohenstaufens now meant nothing. Baroque rockworks lay crumbling in the vineyards; the Mafia, agrarian problems, and, most of all, neglect had depleted the ground and dried up the springs. Paired columns disappeared under the plaster of village reconstructions; a flight of steps led nowhere; the military cap of an uncle killed in the siege of Gaeta hung in a room no one entered; an Algerian rug and leather chairs had, each in turn, ended up as venerable relics. In the same way that a string of owners had remodeled Gemara according to their needs or whims, their vision of grandeur or their peasant stinginess, so had this decrepit house fashioned the last descendant of the family in its own image, this Ruggero di Credo, who was only an heir to that ancient domain.

His farmers, who knew him from birth; his daughters; his wife, who, after all, had loved him when he was still young—none could picture him any way but old. Old age seemed the natural state of this man—he was important only as the end product of the past. At sixteen, Don Ruggero must have looked like a Sicilian youth from a Pindar poem; at thirty, his slender face assumed the expression of dryness and passion found in the Christs of the Martorana mosaics. At sixty, he resembled a Moslem sorcerer in medieval Sicily; it was as if he himself were merely a cracked mirror vaguely reflecting racial ghosts. Bending over his hand, a chiromancer could not have read his palm, because Don Ruggero had no future; perhaps the chiromancer would have read, not Don Ruggero's past, but the past of the two dozen men lined up behind him in death. Don Ruggero's personal life had been virtually nonexistent, but that very void seemed a selfwilled form of immobility. He had been an Italian consul in Biskra; he had ruined his career by marrying, late in life, an unalterably vulgar Jewish Algerian woman with a shady reputation, but this had been for him what the suffering that leads back to God is for the mystic. His retirement put him outside this century; that is to say, in Gemara. So began, for this lunatic, twenty wonderful years, empty as a summer day.

When Rosalia di Credo thought of her father, she pictured him sitting on a pile of stones, a bowl between his knees, eating his soup like a farmhand. Not that Don Ruggero labored to improve his estate; he had better things to do. He discovered treasure, or at least he was going to. The scarcity of water had turned him into a dowser; he had been walking his fields for years, holding in his hands an ash stick that was like a mysterious instrument linking him to his lands. Then the search for springs of water gave way to the search for treasure; no doubt, his ancestors had buried deep down in the ground enough gold to compensate for selling the citrus fruit at a loss and for earning such small dividends on his government bonds. Finally, a chance meeting with an archaeologist made him dream of statues, which for him was a way of dreaming of women. He no longer paid any attention to his wife, usually flopped on pillows and stuffed with food, but rather looked at tanned, barefoot village girls in faded smocks, who would sometimes venture under the trees to where he was, part necromancer, part satyr. Don Ruggero would then let go of his shadowy goddesses to reach for these warm statues of flesh. Animals and trees suffer when thwarted in their labor for man, but it mattered not that his trees, unpruned, ungrafted, suffered because they couldn't bear fruit and his oxen because they weren't put to use; nor did it matter that Gemara was crumbling: he carried within himself these dry lands the wind endlessly sowed with dust, these buried treasures, these empty fountain basins one could have fallen into.

All sorts of scraps of ideas floated in his mind as in dark waters: he remained faithful to the memory of the Sicilian Bourbons and disdained the dynasty of the Savoys: the fall of Papal Rome did not impress him, since this was something that occurred in the north. He scorned money and businessmen but extorted a few pennies from his neighbors who were interested in his dowsing stick; or tried, by refusing to sell, to raise the price of a piece of land no one would have wanted otherwise. This man who seldom washed practiced exquisite refinements, almost ridiculous in their court-liness because they were so out of date, but still they impressed tax collectors and creditors; this penniless man was prodigal with his daughters; this husband, whom Donna Rachele had energetically betrayed as long as her youth and beauty permitted, treated his two girls with a strictness that stemmed less from old-fashioned austerity than from a jealousy bordering on incest. They were not allowed to speak to any man, not even the priest, or the cripple who sold laces on the village square. Yet pride led him to give permission to have Angiola photographed by strangers who had come to visit the ruins of a theater in the low-lying reaches of the country—the only neighborhood site mentioned, though without an asterisk, in the guidebooks about Sicily.

Too poor to follow the custom, he had not been able to send his daughters to a convent in Palermo to be edu-cated. Their studies had consisted of raucous maternal songs, music-hall refrains transformed in their mouths into lovely cantilenas, popular ballads and pamphlets on

39

sexual hygiene lifted from a servant's drawer, and fragments of Greek verse taught by Don Ruggero, who no longer understood them himself. Since all this is not enough to fill a mind, there was plenty of room left for the remembrances that make up childhood: room for the excitement of the village feast and the quasi-ritual confection of anise bread, room for the taste of fresh figs, for the smell of oranges rotting in the garden under piles of palm branches, room for a grove of hazel trees Angiola could wander in barefoot, hanging on a branch the thick cotton socks Don Ruggero's sense of propriety made his daughters wear, room for the death of an owl and the first throbbings of the heart. A world apart, the house had its laws, even its own climate, because it seemed to Rosalia that all she had seen there had been dazzling days. The early return of a migratory bird was taken as a miracle, but people thought it only natural that Santa Lucia cured the blind, or that Salome appeared naked in the sky on Midsummer Night.

On warm evenings, they ate outdoors on the terrace, under a pavilion at the foot of the house, embellished and restored by night light. The woman from the village who served as their maid went home, taking with her the leftovers of the meal. The inexhaustible voice of Don Ruggero replaced that of the fountain, a source of great pride, unheard for years in the garden. He spoke about genealogy with authority, about magic in the tone of one who knew much more than he revealed; when he spoke about Gemara, he became eloquent. The accounts of their present and past riches came out so garbled that time appeared reversible: the girls no longer knew if he was talking about today, tomorrow, or yesterday. They became wealthy, gratified, married to princes; the King himself would take the trouble to come to the dig Don Ruggero would start in the olive grove as soon as he had cleared it of trees. Gemara would regain its former splendor, which had never been lost, since the obstinate old man hadn't stopped dreaming of it. Donna Rachele, asleep in her chair, was explaining for the umpteenth time to her girlfriends from Biskra that she had married a nobleman, a real one, who had been decorated and who had property in Sicily. Leaning on the balustrade and looking at the stars, whose names she did not know, Angiola saw a wondrous wedding veil floating over the void, a veil unrelated to plans for the future or even to the confused emotions of her nubility. Don Ruggero's cheap cigar went out. The old man went up to bed, stopping in the entrance hall to contemplate once more the meager finds so far unearthed in his lands: potsherds, a few corroded coins, a little Venus with doves whose clay face came off in flakes here and there, fragments of a vase clumsily glued back together. He would touch these objects, precious to him, with a solic- itude that revealed a true nobility of soul, and at the same time he would mine the rich resources of dialect to bombard with lewd and comic insults the Superintendent of Antiquities, who had refused to subsidize his diggings.

This precarious way of life collapsed following a skirmish with the village. A rich country man who had refused to lend Don Ruggero some few thousand lire had his best mare drop dead on Credo land. Misfortunes never come singly; this same peasant's wife died of pneumonia, and a few days earlier, their haystacks had burned down. Don Ruggero had the reputation in the region of casting spells; it was thus as natural to blame him for the calamities as it would have been to thank a saint for a godsend. Old stories were dragged out about strange accidents and deaths too sudden not to involve some mystery; like people rummaging in boxes for a knife, everyone searched deep in his memory for a grievance. Husbands who had had occasion to mistrust their wives' virtue, sharecroppers fired by Don Ruggero in the days when he still had sharecroppers, all joined in the accusations of black magic. Even the church itself, in the guise of the local potbellied priest, joined in, leading the procession of shrill-voiced women and squabbling children on the way to storm Gemara one dusty summer evening.

41

'Pig! Traitor! Dog! Accursed devil!'

They came preceded by their shouts, which gave Don Ruggero and Rosalia time to barricade the only door that wasn't bolted all year around. Solid window bars held against the assault but did not necessarily provide protection against bullets and stones. Pushing his daughters into a safe corner, the old man aimed his gun through the chink of a half-open shutter. All his life, he claimed he had aimed for the sky, but his shot hit the priest, who fell to the ground. Then a siege lasting all night was organized. While Donna Rachele, regaining the agility of her dancing days, escaped through an abandoned cistern to run to the next village to seek reinforcements, the two girls, arms around each other, squealed in reply to the barkings of the pack. More intrepid, Rosalia felt the body of her younger sister tremble against her. Yet it wasn't fear but excitement that made them scream. It was one of these nights when everything seemed possible: it would have been easy to kill, easy to die, easy to go from hand to hand like a living prey or a drinking glass. The one thing that seemed impossible, and perhaps the only misfortune that could have occurred, would have been that nothing happen.

'Break your neck! Drop dead of a stroke!' screeched the old women.

'Kill the Evil One! Bleed the devil!' gasped the priest, thinking he was dying.

But his flock lost heart at the sight of his bloodied cassock. Fear deflected their stones. The more cautious began to tell themselves that a sorcerer with a good gun, barricaded in his own house, was not a man to be taken lightly. The exhortations of the wounded priest would not have kept the peasants from leaving had it not been for the crocks full of gold pieces Don Ruggero was rumored to have hidden in his cellars, and the secret lust for the two girls placed out of reach of village covetousness by their rank and the precautions of their father. Beautiful, familiar, irritating, the sisters were constantly seen by the fountain, in stores, in church; one of them already knew how to arouse a man by simply running her tongue over her lips or suddenly lowering her eyes.

Finally, a shutter gave in; a piece of glass hit Rosalia square in the face; the blood, the broken glass, the gray pale dawn invading the room signaled the end of his dream to Don Ruggero, and the downfall of his reign. Twenty years of madness collapsed under the thrust of people who were blind to the invisible edifice they were bringing down, who thought they had attacked only an old stone house. In this Gemara warped by time, only Angiola had felt stifled like a plant growing cramped in the nook of an old wall. The future, knocking now with a hammer at the door, brought her the unexpected turn of events she had been banking on ever since the days when her eyes would follow the dull tourists too anxious to board their bus again on the village square to dally for a look at a beautiful girl. The sun rose: it was that time of day when night is still barely discernible by the length of shadows; the barn that had just gone up in flames sent up its smoke; rising in the sky, it became blue. Suddenly, by way of a few carabineers on horseback, the state irrupted onto this prehistoric scene.

Don Ruggero, whom dawn did not awaken from his dreams, refused to open to these strangers in uniform. Rosalia didn't dare disobey her father; it was Angiola, terrified (now that there was no more danger), who half opened the door, letting them in along with some fresh morning air that dissipated nightmares, and along with a few peasants no longer insulting but peevish instead. They put the wounded priest on Don Ruggero's bed. The brigadier listened with bored indifference to the contradictory depositions. Guarded by the little troupe, Don Ruggero, now a prisoner, started on his way to a cell, to the city, to the twentieth century. Since he had refused the cart of a compassionate neighbor, he had to cross the village's only street on foot. Here the women, now over their rage, came to say goodbye to this old lover with tender and heartrending farewells. Donna Rachele

43

moved indolently, dragging her feet clad in gaudy slippers. Rosalia had bandaged her forehead; her white handkerchief wound tightly around her temples gave her the appearance of a nun. Before leaving, she had gathered a few possessions in one of her mother's shawls. Angiola had no baggage. But if, to follow in this procession, Angiola assumed the disdainful air of a tragic heroine, it was Rosalia who had the soul of one. This awkward girl in her black, dowdy dress worn out in the armholes had one of those hearts that are devoted to family and home in the rites of an unconscious religion and of an undefinable love. Their father, dethroned from his kingdom of madness, chewed the tobacco charitable carabineers had given him; he had no idea that behind him he dragged his Ismene and his Antigone; and his blindness only enhanced the tragic resemblance.

Rosalia hardly remembered Palermo: what stayed in her memory were the walls of the prison where she visited her father, the faded furniture of the apartment the three women rented, and the public garden where at night she walked with Angiola, who would turn around now and then to smile at a stranger; she felt like the shadow of this dazzling girl. Then, after what seemed weeks, or months—for time no longer mattered, since it was now measured by new clocks—Don Ruggero was back to sit beside his fat wife as she stuffed herself with candied fruit. A weak, haggard Don Ruggero, inexplicably reasonably reasonable, was ready to sell Gemara, where he had only harvested disaster. The lack of buyers forced him to accept a compromise; he rented the house to some rich foreigners. Everyone approved his getting rid of an estate he could no longer live on; moreover, everyone thought the old man had been cured of his madness, because, lodged deeper now, it had become invisible. Don Ruggero seemed detached from his land in Sicily because he now placed his hope in the House cemented by blood that his family represented to him. In prison, he remembered distant cousins, holders

44

of one of those famous names even the most uneducated people had heard of; these cousins were wealthy enough to occupy a whole floor in one of the most handsome palaces in Rome. Even though his letters to the Princes of Trapani had not been answered, he counted on their help to rebuild the Credo fortune, of which Gemara was only a symbol in stone. Rosalia was entrusted with selling their meager jewelry to pay for the passage; it was she who, accompanied by her mother, returned to Gemara now encumbered with the new tenants' trunks, in order to pack what was left of their clothes and household goods; finally, she made all the arrangements for their departure.

Donna Rachele vomited throughout the crossing; Don Ruggero obstinately told all the other passengers his life story; Angiola had left the first man she loved in Sicily; to try to cheer her, Rosalia kissed her pale hands sadly. The passionate affection she felt for her sister allowed her to take on the parts of both the lover and the loved. The artless girl failed to realize that the inner constraints of weariness, of stupor, and of vanity block further suffering just when one most suffers, so that Rosalia lent her strength intact to the despair of another person. Had she grieved for herself, certain memories, certain particular regrets would have limited her unhappiness; crying for someone else, the girl unconsciously wept for all the sorrows of love. Angiola fell asleep toward morning; Don Ruggero, oblivious to the humiliations that awaited him in Rome, was snoring in the next berth; Rosalia watched over them as if she were their spirit. She had allowed them to rest all the burdens of their lives on her for so long that she had become like a servant who suffered for them.

For Rosalia, losing her sister was not as painful as leaving Sicily; unhappiness had become a habit. Then, unable to accept the separation, she considered it, like all separations that rend the heart, temporary. Don Ruggero pestered his cousins until they agreed to send Angiola to a boarding school for daughters of noblemen in Florence; in this way, he felt he was silencing those who saw him only as a peasant usurping his own name. Rosalia approved of this plan, which removed her young sister from the vague dangers of the street, from a senile father, from a whimpering mother, and from the discomfort of the crammed apartment Don Ruggero had rented on the top floor of a building on Via Fosca. Angiola was sixteen: candid, hair uncurled now, eyes downcast in an unpowdered face, the morning of her departure she seemed to have retreated back into her childhood; Rosalia understood that her sister had cast aside the real Angiola the way she might cast aside a light dress in autumn to wear it again come spring. She led this little girl dressed in navy blue to the train station; only strangers would have mistaken the child for Angiola.

For three years, in each new affliction, Rosalia found consolation in her sister's absence; Don Ruggero spoke of selling his dowsing secrets for fabulous sums to get back on his feet again and to return to Sicily: Rosalia's life was spent waiting for either her sister's reappearance or the departure for home. Returning from the convent, Angiola seemed invested with new gracefulness and her pronunciation now shamed the still-meridional inflections of her older sister. Rosalia had her hired, without any difficulty, as a companion to the princess Don Ruggero ceremoniously insisted on calling dear cousin to her face, while in private he made fun of her stinginess, her affectation, even her title, which he envied while contesting its authenticity. The Princess of Trapani had a son: Rosalia dreamed of a marriage that would reopen Gemara to all of them. Fortunately, Don Ruggero was not at home when, leaning on her chauffeur's arm, the old woman climbed the three stories to their apartment to make a scene: pocketing a month's pay in advance, Angiola had vanished without giving notice, and probably not unaccompanied. Neither the princess, who probably preferred not to, nor Rosalia, whom Angiola never told, ever knew the real circumstances of this departure. Rosalia hid the mishap

46

from her father. She placed personal announcements in Rome's biggest papers; hearing nothing, she thought at first her sister had killed herself, then later that the mediocre lover Angiola had once had in Palermo had reappeared. Having a faithful heart herself, she believed in fidelity.

It was during those days that Rosalia di Credo took on the ghostly aspect of mourning by which her neighbors would later remember her. She helped her landlady sell devotional articles: exposed to the obscurity of churches, her face took on the rancid shades of wax once akin to honey. Her mother died, acquiring in one day, thanks to the doctor's visit and the ceremonies of extreme unction, more importance in the neighborhood than she had throughout the interminable four years. Playing lotto, Don Ruggero habitually lost the small sums of money his protectors begrudged him; they finally refused him any further help: he was found posted in front of their door, repeating stupidly over and over again the same word and obscene gesture in order to relieve himself of his disdain. The Prince of Trapani had him committed. Rosalia remained alone in the empty apartment she kept because Angiola knew the address. Finally, when Rosalia was beginning to try to get used to her sister's death, Angiola came back one magnificent day in July; it was this day that, from then on, Rosalia thought of whenever someone referred to a beautiful summer.

She did not ask her sister any questions, because her face told her everything. Everything; that is to say, the only important thing: Angiola had suffered. Without knowing what the transgressions were, Rosalia forgave her; she resented only that she had not been accepted as an accomplice. A repentant Angiola had rings under her beautiful eyes; they made Rosalia forget the gay little goat of the Sicilian gardens, and the shy schoolgirl crying on a train platform in Rome: this new sister was her last love. Their time together was like a breathing spell between two sadnesses; that period of her life became so embellished in memory that, looking back, it seemed almost a time of happiness. This tender affection, which she considered pure, unaware that it could have been otherwise, led her to as many concessions as a physical attachment would have. She skimped on household expenses to be able to dress her sister. She sewed clothes for her that, despite their ugliness, Angiola agreed to wear out of a condescension resembling kindness. Rosalia finally learned that when Angiola had become sick, she had taken refuge in a small village near Florence. Short of funds, she had accepted the help of a local notary whom she had met at the house of the Princess of Trapani. As ironic chance would have it, the man concealed the soul of a Don Quixote in the body of a Sancho Panza. Amused by this fat, tender clown, Angiola had not turned down his marriage proposal: he came to see her whenever business called him to Rome; he brought her those superfluous flowers and chocolates she no longer could live without.

Resigned to her sister's lovers when the men were the sort whose attraction she could, in a pinch, understand, Rosalia despised this dullard Angiola couldn't possibly love, and this disdain kept her from hating him. She hid her scorn for the little house Paolo Farina, who had pulled off some good business deals, was building in Pietrasanta; she helped Angiola choose fabrics and furniture; the day after the wedding, Paolo showed his stinginess by asking to see all the bills. She entrusted their small income to her brother-in-law. He made the trip to Sicily for her; sending him away from Angiola, while forcing him to apply his business acumen on their behalf, gave Rosalia one of those cruel pleasures that, in the long run, endears our victims to us. A few months later, Paolo took the night train to Rome to tell her that Angiola had skipped out. She had left the day before with the second tenor of an opera troupe that had just performed *Aida* in a Florence theater; this time, Rosalia felt a pity born of mutual unhappiness for this fat man weeping in his chair.

Rosalia was not yet thirty; yet she seemed old, so much had life tried this woman, who felt she had never lived. She began to prowl around furnished-apartment buildings and train-station neighborhoods, staring at women beautiful or sad enough to have been Angiola. Taking revenge on Gemara for his wife's desertion, Paolo stopped paying the interest on the mortgage. Rosalia quarreled with him when she saw him one evening at the entrance to a café with another woman, who undoubtedly had replaced the absent one. She did not tell herself that her sister, wherever she was, might be happy; Angiola's misfortunes were the only thing that gave her hope. Rosalia expected to find her again, betrayed, maybe sick, but, in any case, downhearted; she would not even inform the grotesque husband who had been responsible for her loss. To earn a living, both of them would work as maids in the family *pension* an Englishwoman had just started in Gemara. But the building seemed to conspire to drive off foreigners; many tenants came and went in a short period of time. The *pension* closed after a few months, with the Englishwoman barely breaking even in the first quarter. Don Ruggero's creditors were losing patience; a newly wealthy flour miller, the worst enemy of the Credos, announced his intention of buying the house, to keep only its four walls and make a modern villa out of what had been Gemara.

Every time she got a summons, Rosalia would go warn her father; she still thought he could save everything. But, mired in torpor, Don Ruggero was becoming as inaccessible as the dead or the gods. He remained seated for hours, mute as a deaf person, sullen as some blind ones, running his hands back and forth on his wicker chair. Rosalia stubbornly went on talking to him, not realizing that words cannot penetrate the soul's deafness. Sometimes, feeling threatened in his peace, the old man would lift his head apprehensively; then a stupid smug expression would blank out his face again; his smile, evident at the corners of his lips and eyes, would express, not pleasure at having understood, but

malicious joy at understanding nothing. Using his clever-
ness as a bow, this sly peasant played on his misfortune
as on a cello. In Sicily, he had used his magic to swindle
his admirers, even his enemies; in Rome, he had black-
mailed his rich relatives with his wretchedness; humi-
lated by a life that had stolen his dreams one after the
other, he hid from failure behind his insanity. Just as he
was sinking, he landed on his island again: madness was
his Sicily. His daughter had not run away with the
second tenor of a small-town troupe; she was still there;
intact as the statues that, thanks to him, had emerged
out of the earth's womb; statues to which he could com-
pare her young naked beauty while she bathed in the
woods in the Roman cistern. These statues, exhumed by
him, had risen to come to him as many women. These
and no others filled the galleries of the Piazza Olivella
Museum in Palermo. And it was shrewd to throw off his
creditors by spreading a rumor that he was bankrupt;
he knew the truth, for in the cellar, in straw baskets
behind empty bins, he had enough gold pieces to restore
Gemara. And this wicker chair (ha, ha!) was a marble
throne he never tired of caressing. Rosalia's presence
irritated the sick man: unrecognized by her father, who,
she said, was no longer himself, she left the asylum
quickly; she didn't see that, like sorcerers who sell their
souls to obtain power over things, this dotard had traded
his mind for his own universe.

The evening church bells were ringing when Rosalia
came home; her landlady had a letter for her that bore a
postmark from Palermo. She waited till she was inside
her room before opening it. Paolo Farina was informing
her that Gemara would be sold at public auction on such
and such a day, through the offices of such and such a
law firm; the black-and-white paper was like the official
announcement of her own death. She sat down on the
bed, looking with distant eyes at this room, where
things—the floor, the furniture—seemed adrift like
flotsam: the easy chair, which was superfluous, since

Don Ruggero would never sit in it anymore; the bed Angiola would never lie in again. Rosalia had resigned herself to these losses in her very despair over them, but Gemara, she had thought, would always be safe in her mind. She had almost accepted the idea of never going back, as long as, if it was raining in Rome in February, she could imagine the sun on those stone terraces. She finally understood in some vague way, as those who think with their hearts understand, that that realm would no longer exist a few hundred miles away but years away; the house was her past. The demolition of Gemara would take place only in her heart, because stones don't feel the striking of the pick; her father was too old to suffer, and Angiola no longer gave it a thought. A newly rich flour miller had the right to raze Gemara, because, if the family ever went back, the mirror would not recognize them. She herself had unconsciously torn down and rebuilt those old walls: the luxurious Gemara she had wished her sister, the princely Gemara she wished her father as revenge against the scorn of fashionable people—those had nothing in common with the dwelling of her childhood, which no longer existed even in her, for her dreams had adulterated her memories. Better still, right now this calamity did not affect her completely: a piece of the cracked mirror over her bed gave her back the image of a person who would have liked nothing better than to keep on cooking and selling votive candles had she been allowed to do so. The darkness slowly unburdened her of this stranger who was none other than herself. She took a few steps in her room; its walls no longer protected her from the void. She was not surprised suddenly to feel, as though it were any ordinary physical need, a desire to die.

Stifled by unhappiness as by sudden asphyxiation she quickly opened the window. The sounds of Rome, composed of invisible comings and goings on the quiet street, broke over her like a wave. She felt cold, although the heavy air heralded summer. Set up on a series of balconies of all sizes, and wherever the roof jutted out, skimpy gardens were watered at night by women in pincurls and in house dresses. Three flights down, in the courtyard of a neighboring house, a woman seen from the back was feeding pigeons; her arms, covered with wings, evoked for Rosalia the arms of the little clay idol found in fragments under their garden in Sicily.

'Ma-da-ma Cel-la!'

'Aaah-hi! How you startled me!'

Marcella had turned her head to see who was calling her. The pigeons flew off. Heavy as marble, her beautiful face was calm. Yet she had been frightened, but by the fear, alert and quickly controlled, felt by those for whom danger is an old habit.

'What do you want?'

'Some glowing embers please, Madama Cella. A little more. I put the money in the basket.'

The basket came down attached to a rope; in it was the obol for Charon in the form of a ten-lira coin bearing the effigy of a monarch from the House of Savoy. Marcella went inside, then came back out carrying a receptacle in her hands. She was accustomed to doing these little favors, which are compulsory courtesies among neighbors. The basket was weighed down by an iron receptacle; in it, coals from dead forests were just lit by pine cones from living ones. The basket went up slowly, hitting against gutter ledges here and there; Rosalia pulled on the rope as if she were hauling in her death.

'Anything else?'

'Nothing for the time being, Madama Cella.'

'Just a moment then, I'll go get your change.'

'Later, Madama Cella. Good night.'

'Good night.'

She closed the windows, the blinds, the curtains. In the room carefully insulated against the outside air, the sounds of Rome were now only the confused clamor of waves, the imperceptible trepidation of machines you can still sense even in a tightly shuttered cabin. Rosalia sat down on her trunk; it was now out of the question to send it anywhere; leaning over the small stove, she fanned it with the papers from the notary. When one is cold, one should try to get warm. In the middle of the sea, it is always cold. The acrid coal smell reminded her of the steamboat between Palermo and Naples: she was sitting on the trunk in a second-class cabin; the noise— that was her father snoring in the next berth. She had been crazy to expect Angiola to return here; the child had been waiting for her in Sicily for ages. The smell of something burning—that was the corn harvest burning in the barn: the barn was so big that it had been burning for twelve years. Palermo was twelve hours away from Naples: they would not arrive before dawn. Flames began to leap; the hem of her merino skirt, touching the lit embers, caught fire; she wasn't afraid, but the flames had to be extinguished. If they were not, the whole of Gemara would catch fire. These weren't votive-candle flames; she never lit a candle to be granted a wish: too often, the same wretched people bought them at Santa Maria Minore; she no longer believed in their usefulness. She put her hands on her skirt to tamp down the flames: a vague desire came over her to roll on the bed to stifle them; but the smoke, thickening like fog, was already choking her. Rosalia crossed the room; it rolled and pitched under her; her heart capsized by deadly seasickness, she fell on the bed.

People were knocking on the door: she heard but did not want to open to these torch-bearing peasants. She was suffocating, but it was wiser not to open the window. She had forgotten that she wanted to die. Images followed one another in her darkened head, probably no less numerous or lively than usual, but explained differently. She was tired: that was not at all strange after a sleepless night in the besieged house. Luckily, dawn would soon come. The iron bed, the bark, slipped away with such even speed that it no longer made her dizzy. The bedspread, then the mattress, ignited: firelight played on the whitewashed wall like the first redness of morning in the gray sky of dawn.

'St. Anthony! What hellish smoke!'

She did not hear. Alerted by the smell, her neighbors on the right tried to break down the door; it gave way, and they entered the room. She did not hear them stream pitchers of water everywhere, put out the fire, cough, open the window, and share the excitement of the discovery with the neighbors on the second floor. Peaceful, lying like the corpses of her ancestors on funeral pyres on her charred bedspread, eyes wide open, Rosalia di Credo had just reached the foot of a nocturnal, monstrous Gemara; Angiola was waiting for her.

'This way. I'll go call her.'

'You see, I'm in a hurry. Since I live in Ostia . . .'

He had guessed who she was even though she had not given him her name. This too properly dressed woman was probably not affiliated with the group. Besides, for some weeks now, the members of the group had gone underground. A customer would have come in through the shop door. Yes, it really was this woman whose picture Carlo had shown him one day. Moreover, her black-gloved hands were trembling.

'Come in. We can't talk in this hallway. And besides, people walking by can hear.'

Compromised already, she followed him into a kitchen also used as a place to sleep in, since it had a bed. It was dark in the room. He turned on the light with the kind of assurance one has in one's house. The power, sent from the Terni Cascades to be transformed into light here, showed to advantage the almost too delicate, quasi-perfect, but anxious face of the young man; his expression was forever at odds with his beauty. He noticed the black handbag, the black coat, the scarf, like a widow's veil, framing unflatteringly the drawn features of the visitor. Grotesque, he thought. A little bourgeois woman in mourning.

'They ate everything, Massimo,' said a warm feminine voice from the other side of the partition. 'You know? They walk on my hands, they even take the grains from my lips. And what strength in their little pink claw grip. But you know, I don't really matter. If by chance

55

tomorrow a neighbor was to . . .'

'Come on,' he said impatiently, raising his voice. 'We're waiting for you.'

The warning was lost in a noise of shutters being closed. Marcella's footsteps were approaching on the tile floor.

'My little pigeon,' she said, cooing a tender slangy expression. 'Why did you turn on the lamp? I still have so many things to tell you. It's better in the dark.'

The visitor blushed as though she were spying on a naked woman. Surprised but in no way disconcerted, Marcella stopped on the threshold. Since she was some distance from the lamp, her face was not clearly visible.

'Marcella,' said the young man, approaching to close the door behind her, 'Madama Stevo is here, perhaps for news.'

He knew her name? Vanna's hands shook even more. She took her gloves off without thinking. Indeed, her intentions were simple. She planned to keep the visit matter-of-fact, carefully avoiding any show of emotion. For reasons opposed to her own, these people considered her presence there quite natural; they were as comfortable with their tragic sincerity, whose banality they ignored, as Vanna was with her own conventions, whose inanity she was likewise unaware of. And with the gesture of someone getting ready to leave: 'It's Madama Marcella I'd like to speak with,' she said.

'Massimo Iacovleff wouldn't be here if he didn't know everything. He's'—she hesitated—'Signor Stevo's closest friend.'

The stubborn, almost insulting look of the visitor made her correct herself. 'Carlo's closest friend,' she said, 'our Carlo.' And softly, with an affectionate simplicity: 'Poor man.'

Unwittingly, she was speaking of him as if he were dead.

They sat down. Everything was arranged as if to evoke a ghost: the half-light, the smoke spread by Massimo's cigarettes, their hands placed on the table as for a séance. But the spirit evoked was different for each one. Vanna thought of the convalescent leaning on her during their walks in Ostia, of the great man reassured by the little comforts of middle-class life, of her marital happiness which, vanishing as quickly as a dream, had left her stranded in the midst of a complicated world she had never fully understood. Marcella was reliving the glorious plans discussed with childish daring and melodramatic precautions, of a trip to Geneva on which sympathizers had helped them cross the border, of pamphlets slipped under doors in the early hours of the morning, of the shame and despair that overwhelmed them as, sitting side by side, in this very room, they listened to the dictator's voice thundering on the radio, of the frantic activity that prevented them from sleeping when, worn with fatigue, they lay down fully dressed on the bed, not as lovers, but as accomplices. Massimo saw again in a café in Vienna a stranger in threadbare clothes for whom he had procured a false visa on a false passport, a sick man extraordinarily alive who, while pressing his wrists with damp hands, the hands of a tuberculosis patient, enthusiastically stammered in shaky German his ideas on life, his secret projects, and hazy avowals of affection. Of so many Carlos, one separated from them by space, the others by time, it was the first one they were unwittingly sacrificing. None of them could fully imagine what might be the life of this prisoner at the very moment when they were talking. And like the faithful, for whom their gods have to be not only real but unique, each of the three ignored or scorned the ghost that haunted the other; each was absorbed in his own silent contemplation.

'Does anyone know? Perhaps he'll return soon,' Vanna ventured shyly.

'Never,' said Marcella contemptuously.

The possibility of a moment of indulgence, of humanity perhaps, coming from the dictator scandalized her, worried her like a dangerous spiritual temptation that might risk weakening her indignation and therefore her hatred.

Marcella Ardeati was born in Romagna, in Cesena, where her mother worked as a midwife. Her father, a militant anarchist, had been deprived of his teaching job by order of the despot, who had once been his childhood friend. A young, rich, famous doctor had married her for love after a stormy affair of a few months, during which she had, by turn willingly and unwillingly, given herself. She had left him two years later, blushing at this advantageous marriage as if it were a criminal attachment, which it was, since those passionate years had sidetracked her from her true vocation; that is, from tragic reality. Wealth, success, pleasure, happiness itself provoked in her a horror analogous to that felt by the Christian for the flesh. In the same way that the Christian cannot fully enjoy bodily pleasures, since shame and guilt spoil his enjoyment, so pleasure and money for Marcella had brought back the memory of her father miserably dying in a common hospital ward in Bologna and of her mother condemned for having induced abortions. This solidarity with the suffering of her parents had gradually allied her to all those humiliated, oppressed, punished. The expectation of the future had given this woman, committed to rebellion, the large eyes of young Sibyls. She had met Carlo Stevo at the very moment when both were most desperate about the state of their country and the world. This exasperated man, fragile yet daring to press his ideas to the limit so that they became actions, had found in her a violent Martha and at the same time a mystical Mary. For this Slav from Trieste who had adopted Italy with a passion, she had been the earth, the powerful Italian earth that survived the chaos of whatever regime. She represented the People for this loner from a good, liberal, middle-class family, one of the very families that had invented the concept of the People but whom a remnant of custom, of prejudice and fear prevents from mixing freely with the Masses. Perhaps for Carlo Stevo she represented, even more easily, popular simplicity and strength, since because of her education, her marriage, and her friends, Marcella was no longer entirely of the People. While this misogynous, this shy, or perhaps chaste, man hadn't treated her as a woman, a common hatred rather than pleasure bound them together. He had moved in, the year before he was deported; in her grain store, between bags full of feed, they held secret meetings with their friends, incubating, in this Rome once again imperial, the pure fanaticism of young persecuted sects. It was in this room that he was arrested soon after his return from Vienna. But whereas the sense of justice, of right, and his aroused impersonal kindness had led Carlo to hate the new master who personified the State, it was, on the contrary, hate that little by little had led this woman, friend of all losers, to feel the stirrings of kindness. Everything about Marcella irritated Vanna: her handsome, worn, somewhat coarse face; her big, tired hands; her breasts unconstrained under her black wool shawl.

Hurrying to speak before anger stifled her, she said: 'We haven't had news of him for three months. I'm not in the habit of visiting strangers . . . but I thought . . .' She was panting as though she'd had to climb a steep hill. 'I told myself that perhaps you had connections we don't have . . . If by chance you had a message for me . . .'

'Carlo does not write to us either,' said Marcella.

'Oh?'

Vanna looked at her unbelievingly, with suspicion, yet willing to think that her rival was not treated better than herself.

'If they contain anything but trifles, letters are intercepted,' said Marcella firmly. 'I don't see Carlo writing to say that the weather is nice and that he is feeling fine.' She got up to take a coffee pot and two empty cups off the table, showing by these house-keeping moves that she wasn't interested in the visit.

'But he's not well. Don't you remember that he was spitting blood? Who knows if at this very moment he is still among us, poor man!'

'You didn't imagine they'd send him back to us alive?'

'I'm sure that would bother you,' Vanna suddenly screamed out. 'To think that I thought that you loved him as much as I do,' she added, rising like a woman on the point of striking or slapping someone. 'I almost felt sorry for you . . . I told myself: this woman is like me, she is suffering . . . I should hate her but I almost felt sorry for her . . . I had my hair done to go see her . . . I didn't know I would be dealing with some factory worker wearing a shawl . . . A man like him, a man who always made you feel you weren't dressed elegantly enough, you weren't refined enough for him . . . And look at her, the pig, unconcerned as if it hadn't been her fault that all this happened . . .'

Then, with an unexpected, studied insolence that was surprising coming from her: 'Forgive me, sir, for speaking of your friend like this in front of you.'

'Don't worry about me, Madama Stevo,' the young man said softly.

'I suppose you would have protected him. You would have walled him in with a proper middle-class life? You would have advised him to make his peace with the Ruler, to write nice books, nice novels, something to pay for a little trip to Paris each year, a holiday in the Alps, or a new car. Don't I know how these marriages work? You would have used his illness to stifle the rebel in him, the hero, the apostle. Carlo always told me that his marrying you was one of the worst things that came of his pneumonia.'

'He told you that? You?'

'Who else would he say it to? Who else cares about his marriage?' Separated by the table, hands on the shiny oilcloth, the two women confronted each other in fury; they were like coarse fatal symbols of Carlo's fate—he had struggled between them, in vain, like a swimmer caught between a mudbank and a rock. And (because hatred is the most melodramatic of passions) the middle-class housewife spoke like a slut and the lower-class one spoke like an actress.

Overwhelmed, Marcella sat down again. 'I'm really too good to bother with you,' she said. 'Get her out of here, Massimo, tell her to go . . .'

She closed her eyes for a moment, trying to blank out everything but one brilliant cold, hard object. When I was a nurse in Bologna, working with Alessandro, I would help him extract a bullet from the lungs or the belly of the wounded, she told herself; here I must do the opposite. Shoot this thing, destroy it, make a hole in this bag full of blood. Nothing else matters. Don't work yourself up: this is not the time for trembling hands. Dead or alive, Carlo, there is a secret between us that would make this silly woman blanch; what you could barely wish would be done, I will accomplish. You, you're only a dreamer.

'Exactly, I nursed him,' said Vanna Stevo almost softly, going back to what Marcella had said earlier. 'I know that he is weak—all men are cowards—and he's afraid of death . . . I'm not the one who compromised him; I didn't get involved in politics; I didn't lead him to his downfall to get rid of him. Did you ever think of Carlo himself? And did you ever think of the child? And me, did you ever think of me waiting for him, stuck in the house with no one ever ringing the doorbell, not even the mailman? My mother saying her rosary, consulting the cards to see if disaster is on the way . . . My father coming home late at night complaining that business is bad, he only has money for his English bitch . . . A family beyond reproach, which now is ashamed because of me when flags are paraded in the street . . . Holy Virgin,' she went on with a shy woman's violence, 'do you think that's being alive? At least, if I could forget Carlo, I could find someone else . . . Or if I were a different kind of woman . . . And here I am tonight, and I find you with your lover . . .'

'How ridiculous,' cried Marcella, with a short, strained laugh.

'Your boarder?'

'I don't rent rooms anymore,' Marcella said scornfully.

'Leave her alone, she's suffering,' whispered Massimo to his friend. And turning to the enemy, he pushed back the strip of newspaper where, to do something, he had been drawing circles, squares, palm trees. 'Carlo often spoke of you, my dear, at the time we met in Vienna. He would say, "Vanna is beautiful and she doesn't know it." He was planning to put the child in a sanatorium in Oetztal. How is she doing?'

'And if she learned to crawl on crutches, would my cross be any lighter? He couldn't even make me a child who could walk like everybody else,' she said, half sneering, half plaintively. In the presence of these people who seemed to think aloud, she also seemed, in turn, to open up, to admit things she never could have to her own family. She was unable to love this little girl on whom she was spending all her money for toys and doctors; all this care and bother she took was a way of hiding to herself her shame at having formed, of her own flesh, this sickly little cripple. Sometimes, in the early-morning hours, lying on her bed next to the cage-like bed of the invalid, she felt a desperate, sharp, horrible desire to stifle the child under a pillow, and then kill herself.

'My husband is the one who is treating her, right?' asked Marcella, almost tenderly. 'That's how I met Carlo . . . God, how long ago it all seems . . .'

'Carlo is very low, very depressed,' Massimo suddenly said. 'He has just written the Ruler to retract what he calls his errors.'

'It's not true!'

'It's true, Marcella, it's in the evening newspapers.'

'You believe their lies?'

'They showed me the letter.'

'Who?'

But she grabbed the newspaper that was lying on a corner of the table.

'It's true,' repeated Massimo, putting his hand on her shoulder. 'Almost everything is true. The advice you gave him seemed to have been followed, Madama Stevo.'

Vanna quickly took the newspaper Marcella had

dropped, and moved closer to the lamp to read it. A pink blush appeared on her cheeks, while the other woman's were drained of all color.

'Massimo,' whispered Marcella, 'how long have you known this?'

'Since this morning.'

'Why didn't you say anything?'

'I felt sorry for you.'

'He really gave them names? Whose?'

'Two or three already compromised names. Don't worry: his letter will cause them more embarrassment than us harm. Don't make things worse, Marcella,' he went on, watching the woman, who went on reading. 'Give up what you're thinking; his position could be atrocious, don't aggravate it. Wait until we know what's up before doing anything.'

'I didn't say anything.'

'You're more transparent than you think.'

Radiant, Vanna folded the newspaper, opened her purse, and taking out her makeup, started to make herself beautiful again, like a woman about to go out to meet someone. Poor woman, thought Massimo, she thinks she'll see him again soon.

Again, if only for a moment, Marcella withdrew, head in her hands. 'I don't blame you. It doesn't matter with what tortures, with what promises ... Their worst crime: they make us dirty, they find a way to make us bend or appear to do so, they manage so that no one remains unsoiled. All the more reason for me to act without delay. For revenge, as expiation ... For the party, for you, Carlo, for myself ... We're all more or less fragile tools, that's all. You can't blame a tool for breaking.'

The doorbell made her jump. 'Already!'

'I'm sure that's not it,' said Massimo. 'But let me see.'

'I don't want them to find you here,' she said, grabbing him by the arm. 'Get out of here. Leave through the bedroom!'

'Why?'

But he obeyed, vaguely shrugging his shoulders. She pushed him into an adjoining room which Carlo used to stay in and from which one could leave through the back shop. Vanna sneered at this sort of stage business.

The doorbell rang for the second time impatiently. It isn't them, Marcella thought, they wouldn't ring like that. As soon as the door was opened, she stepped back with a little scream, surprised, almost afraid, but in a different way from her perpetual state of alert; her fear seemed to emanate from a different part of herself. Not watching, the visitor tripped on the steps leading from the entrance down to the half-sunken kitchen. The man was in evening clothes, but he was so at ease that he did not appear ridiculous in this catacomb-like atmosphere.

'They're no longer renting rooms,' Vanna said with insolence.

'My husband,' Marcella said, pronouncing this word as Vanna would have in her place, with a sort of vulgar, almost defiant ostentation.

'If he's got secrets to tell, I would advise him to speak low.' Vanna left, slamming the door.

'Who is that crazy woman?'

'You know her: she's Carlo Stevo's wife,' said Marcella scathingly. She then turned her defiance on him.

'I've arrived right in the middle of a crisis . . . Perfect timing for a doctor. May I sit down?'

'Yes.'

'Am I disturbing you?'

'Yes.'

Hands leaning on the table, she was, unwittingly, standing like a defendant. Dr. Alessandro Sarte sat down, dropping his smile as was his custom in his office at the beginning of the kind of inquest that an examination is. 'You're beside yourself . . . What did that witch tell you?'

'Nothing. She came for news.'

'And did you give her some?'

64

'I only know what's in the evening papers. You've come to gloat, I suppose? You intend to observe the effect of this disaster on me. Well, it's no disaster. You can leave reassured that I'm not in pain.'

'I've better reasons to see you,' he said.

'I don't want to know what they are.'

'Well, I want you to. But first,' he went on, leaning over to touch her with his fingers, 'let me be sure that the Marcella I know is still alive.'

At this simple touch, she jumped back as though he had hit her.

'Calm yourself . . .' Without meaning to, he spoke in the tone of a doctor irritated because his patient moves away just when he is about to be given a shot. 'I didn't intend to take you by surprise . . . Did you ever wonder, in these four years, what had become of me?'

'I didn't have to: you managed to make enough noise with your name. You are on your way to becoming what you wanted: the famous doctor millionaires and celebrities obligatorily call in case of need. You attended conferences; your photograph appeared prominently in *The Fascist Medical Journal, Year X:* you operated on an important member of the party, which allegedly granted you the invaluable favor of the big man himself. Is that it? I suppose your bank account increased tenfold in four years.'

'I don't see why you can't congratulate me for living like a workman from the labor of his hands. The hands of a virtuoso,' he added in the ironic tone of someone reciting some hackneyed phrase; he spread his hands before him on the oilcloth.

Marcella barely glanced at them. 'It's this virtuosity that I hate,' she said very fast, hurrying to speak as if words were a barricade against him. 'Science doesn't interest you. Mankind . . .'

'Spare me your big words.'

'I'm not disputing your talents, Alessandro, I was witness to them myself. But your patients are only clients who afford you an opportunity to triumph or the excuse

65

to experiment.' She went on bitterly: 'Experimenting with the human body is your favorite pastime, even excluding surgery.'

'Let's not oversimplify everything, Marcella. With the human body, yes, and sometimes also with the human soul.'

Elbows on the table, his face leaning on the palms of his hands, he took in, without seeming to, the furniture and the objects in the room. Dr. Sarte had an impassive yet changeable face that constituted a succession of masks: there was the physician's mask, tense in attentiveness, which was not solely his but was used by many of his colleagues; there was a meridional mask, with the features found on Roman coins, a mask worn by the entire race for two thousand years; and then, more personal because it was more secretive, there was the mask of the voluptuary, hinted at from the edges of the other masks. Finally, in those rare moments when Alessandro thought he was alone, or when he forgot to put up his guard, his real face appeared, a hard face with a bitter, cold, distressed look he concealed in life but would probably wear in death.

'Yet,' she said, her voice shaking, 'my own soul doesn't seem to interest you.'

'Don't be so sure of it! To tell you the truth, the word is outdated in my vocabulary as well as yours. Keep talking about me, Marcella. My life story amuses me.'

'What's left to say?' she went on, seizing the opportunity to unleash her anger. 'Last year you hunted at Grosseto with royalty. You smashed up, or traded in, or sold two or three sports cars. You slept here and there with whatever pretty girls were available. You had two or three mistresses from among those flashy women wrapped in mink whose names people whisper in restaurants and theaters as they walk past. You spoiled them, used them; you tired of them . . .'

'A compliment to you.'

'You sought certain sensations from them, including danger. Come to think of it, your women represent the

66

same thing in your life as your Bugattis.'

'A way of getting there, what else?'

'Yes . . . which explains why I soon got tired of being used as a vehicle.'

He noted, as a small victory, that she was beginning to smile. After a moment, exploiting the subject, he went on: 'Speaking of Bugattis, I see you haven't forgotten the evening you chose to go on to San Marino on foot.'

'I don't want to kill myself for nothing.'

'You reassure me,' he said, serious now. And rising, he took a few steps in silence in the room.

'Do you know that, eyes closed, I'd recognize you from your way of speaking, even if you disguised your voice? I can hear the influence of nineteenth-century poets, those profound imbeciles that cluttered up your father's mind and library, and whom you thought to find again in Carlo; my own influence taught you clarity at least, and . . . you haven't changed a bit, Marcella.'

'I wouldn't say the same for you. You've aged.'

'I've worn myself out. Believe me, those who age don't wear themselves out; they preserve themselves. To wear out is the opposite of aging. Do you smoke?'

'No.'

'I see: cured of my vices. And what is this ashtray full of ashes doing here?'

'Don't waste your detective talents on such small stuff,' she said, putting the ashtray in the sink. 'I had lunch with a friend.'

'The Iacovleff kid?'

'You have me watched? What solicitude!'

'I watch over you. It's more necessary than you think. Listen,' he went on, ignoring her protests, 'how do you think you've been able to live more or less in peace, seemingly free, with the ideas and the friends you're known to have? At least give me credit for not having imposed myself on you these last four years.'

'I see,' she said bitterly. 'I would be out on Lipari, were it not . . . What I wonder is, what's behind this kindness.'

She was sitting down again. Arms crossed, elbows on the table, chin lowered, she had become a closed and hard surface to the eyes.

'Nothing but my reluctance to see a woman end her days in the salt mines . . . Especially my own wife,' he added with softness, loosening his mask. 'Since our laws fortunately don't recognize divorce. And, without pretending that I think of you more often than I do, I admit that from time to time I wonder if I played my cards right . . .'

'Of course. You could have done better than to marry your nurse.'

'My best nurse. No one has yet come close to you, Marcella.'

'Is that an offer of a job?'

'No, of course not,' he said, countering her irony with exasperation. 'Neither is it an invitation to come back to the conjugal nest. Do you think I enjoyed that mixture of good times and trying ones, those outbursts of virtue, of the romantic pulp heroine, those class rancors brought to bed . . .'

'You liked it all well enough to make me the Signora Sarte,' she said.

'I know,' he said. 'I miscalculated, thinking marriage would make a woman settle down . . . When I think of all the family problems that decision brought me . . . Let it go . . . And even admitting that I was sometimes ineptly demanding or stupidly clever . . . You too connived, Marcella. I fully realize that if I hadn't been in a position to do something for your father, that embittered failure you pass off as a great man, the ceremony would not have tempted you.'

'And you did nothing for him,' she interrupted.

'After his dismissal, no. I never committed myself to doing so.'

'And I guess it was to make me settle down,' she said in a voice that was growing dangerously strident, 'that the day after the ceremony, as you call it, the minute we arrived in Cannes, you inflicted one of your former

68

mistresses on me, that awful, overpainted French-woman we met on the Croisette.'

'Another compliment,' he said, lapsing back into the light tone of a man completely at ease. 'There are few wives one is in such a hurry to introduce to mistresses.'

'Enough, Alessandro!' she said sharply, with aching sadness. 'Let's not reduce the past to pitiful bedroom squabbles . . . Politics drove us apart, that's all. Before that, I thought I loved you.'

'No, no,' he said. 'Politics between a man and a woman is never more than a pretext. You knew me. I wasn't foolish enough not to enroll in the party. Besides, all hypocrisy notwithstanding, I rather admire this for-mer mason who's trying to build up a nation. Nothing is more despicable than the adulation of success, but since success is always fleeting, I'm only anticipating that time in history when this man, like all winners, will figure as a great loser . . . Meanwhile, I don't deny bestowing on practical results my temporary esteem . . . Aren't you the least bit impressed by this man who made it?'

'You forget that I saw how he made it,' she said with scorn. 'My father used to correct his first articles on the glories of socialism.'

'Believe me, Marcella, doctrines one betrays are like women one abandons; they're always in the wrong. Was I going to compromise my hard-won position to fly to the aid of a handful of fanatics like your father or of visionaries like Carlo Stevo? One of the lessons experi-ence taught me is that losers earn their defeat. But an objective view of political necessity is hardly what one can expect from the mistress of a martyr.'

'I've never been Carlo Stevo's mistress.'

'I thought so . . . Don't you think I know Carlo Stevo? No one is more qualified than I to deliver his funeral oration this night.'

'What?'

'Yes,' he said. 'Carlo Stevo died on the island of Lipari about twenty-four hours ago.'

'And you didn't even have the courage to tell me the news straight out,' she said indignantly. 'They killed him?'

'The word hardly applies to a sick man with no more than half a year to live. Say, rather, a form of suicide.'

He waited for a reaction, but there was none. Then: 'He had what he wanted,' he said, partly making up for the harshness of his remark by the tone of his voice. 'He . . . He was a dreamer, the word explains it all for me; I know facts are not to be trifled with. Someone like Stevo could play only one role well, the role of a martyr. But, in a way, the news moves me. We were friends before . . . I can see how a woman could love this enthusiast who saw the world through his heart . . . If you had asked for my advice,' he went on, irritated by her long silence, 'I would have told you that you can't turn someone like Stevo into a man of action, any more than a swan can be turned into a bird of prey. Since he met you, even on his many trips abroad when he got away from you a little, friends said they saw something artificial in him, that he stopped being himself . . . He did his best to be the hero you wished him to be . . . When you're being watched by the regime, you don't agree to come home to work up God knows what ridiculous coup d'état . . . And you don't divulge your plans, in a weak, unguarded moment, to a young Czech or Russian boyfriend you meet by chance in a Viennese restaurant—a friend who, by the way, is a double agent.'

'That's not true!'

'Not that he suspected as much. After all, Carlo wasn't stupid . . . But . . . He let you involve him in your plots, more than happy, I guess, to escape the need to think . . . You pushed him into a corner so that he was obliged to act; now he could let himself slide willingly toward the catastrophe . . . As for the boy you so generously welcomed, who hurried to join him back in Rome (I followed the whole thing quite closely), I am willing to believe that gathering information at your expense was not his sole aim . . . One can't be around Carlo for long without loving him. One can't be around you either without loving you. If the charming kid didn't warn you that the trap was closing in, perhaps it was because there was no more time. And how could he admit to those he loved that he had at first betrayed them? . . . And your dear Massimo needed the police money to support a mistress.'

'That's not true! That's not true!'

'I assure you . . . A little woman with a rather faded look . . . One of my patients . . . That shocks you? . . . It would be funny if you were in love with him.'

'Is that all?' she asked sarcastically. 'Let's get back to Carlo Stevo's death. If you have more details, don't hide them from me.'

'I would advise you not to let your imagination run away with you,' he said, avoiding an answer. 'I'm telling you what I was told.'

She made no reply. He ventured to take her hand for a moment. 'I had a phone call a little while back. I was getting ready to go to the reception at the Balbo Palace. I thought it better that it be me who . . .'

'Thanks,' she said, trying to sound scornful, but unable to stifle the onrush of tears.

'Well, my dear, and I thought you would not forgive him his retraction.'

'They wrung that letter out of him,' she screamed. 'They took advantage of a weak moment, the lapse of a dying man . . . Don't you see that everything has been erased, explained, paid for. Why don't you just go and be a big success insulting our martyrs at the Balbo Palace.'

'Let's put an end to this,' he said scathingly, exasperated by both her ready-made language and her genuine grief. 'Don't be obstinate. Don't make this wretched man into some kind of hero. You admitted yourself that you were never lovers . . . Now you're alone . . . Night and day . . . Let me tell you that there isn't one minute of our life together that I regret, even the quarrels, even the scenes. Oh,' he continued in a lower voice still, carried away by the desire to wrench her away from Carlo's ghost, 'forget the platitudes, the ideas, the parties, the books . . . Do you remember our first date, a fall Sunday in Reggiomonte . . . You loved me that day . . .'

'I was crazy about you.'

'Same thing.'

He leaned toward her, taking the familiar face in his hands, lifting it, drawing it to him as though to kiss it, impelled not so much by a sudden desire as by the determination to get this unmanageable woman to bend. She rose, shoving back her chair, which toppled, pulling the cord from the lamp. She moved away, more on her guard against her body, consenting in spite of herself, throbbing like a heart, than against him; she leaned on the wall, not bending down to pick up her shawl, which had fallen on the floor.

'Stay where you are,' she said in a hard voice.

'Are you afraid? Afraid of yourself?' he asked.

'I'm still in love with you,' she said. 'I'm ashamed of it, but I still love you. And you know it. But it's all over between us.'

Their mutual confession left them embarrassed and uncomfortable with each other. She righted the chair and felt along the wall for the light switch. He moved nearer the bed; above it was a religious print doubtless put up on the wall by the previous tenants, and in front of it a small lamp, unexpected in this spot, in this room. It shone in the night like a paradoxical star.

'Is this where you sleep?'

She nodded. Leaning over the bed, he slowly ran his hand along the blanket as if following the contours of a body. Marcella trembled under this caress which stirred a memory. Suddenly the doctor's fingers found a metallic object hidden under the pillow. She rushed to him to tear it out of his hands.

'Well, well,' he said. 'That's the one that disappeared from my desk in Reggiomonte . . . Is it loaded?'

72

'In any case, not meant for you,' she said.

'A precaution? That's not like you.'

She didn't say anything. He noticed that her face had become very white.

'I seem to remember that, convinced no doubt that the party had to be served to the end, you used to pompously condemn suicide . . .'

'I don't condemn it any longer,' she said. 'Too many people are driven to it. But it's true that there are better ways of dying.'

'So?'

She did the only thing he wasn't expecting: she looked at the clock. Suddenly he remembered, with a panic of foreboding, a pamphlet old Ardeati had written in defense of an oppressed people's right to political assassination. Uncertain—or rather, sure of her answer beforehand—he hesitated to question this Medusa lest he change into a firm intention what was perhaps only a passing thought. He risked only: 'For . . . ?'

'Yes,' she said. 'Tonight. While he's speaking from the balcony of the Balbo Palace.'

He started forward to take the gun from her, but she put it in a drawer of the table and locked the drawer. He gave up almost instantly.

She's setting a trap for me, he thought. I'm not fooled. If it were true, she wouldn't tell it.

'It's stupid,' he said.

'I know you'll do nothing to interfere with my plans,' she went on. 'Admit it, destruction fascinates you. You're too curious about the human soul, as you say, not to want to know if I'll go all the way or not. And, moreover, you would feel like a fool calling the police to say your wife is going to kill Julius Caesar in an hour.'

'I'm not Caesar's keeper. Do you know how to shoot?'

'Don't you remember?'

They both smiled.

'A guard will grab you by the arm; the shot will miss or hit some bystander in the crowd. Tomorrow the newspapers will praise his courage in the face of danger.

They'll stiffen the regulations against some poor devils who will pay for your grand gesture . . . A few foreigners will be kicked out . . . Is that what you want? Are you so set on being shot, point blank, by a guard, or knocked senseless, or beaten to death in a police station?'

'What an inconvenience for you!' she said. 'After all, I officially bear your name.'

She's crazy, he thought, she's crazy and right now she hates me. I mustn't push her too far. Indeed, my name . . .

'Do you think Carlo Stevo would have approved?'

'Yes.' She thought for a moment, then added: 'It doesn't matter.'

He understood then that she couldn't be persuaded any more than an object, a tool or a weapon, could be persuaded. The comparison is senseless, he told himself. She's not an instrument: the idea comes from her.

'How long have you been planning this?'

'Sometimes it seems to me that I have been planning this always.'

Play for time, he thought. A tension like this can't last. It will crumble in a few hours. Unless . . . Stay with her . . . Hold her back against her will . . . No. A terrible temptation came over him, a temptation that was so strong because, for him, the Establishment was only a reality one accepts but does not honor. Could it really be that tonight *something* would happen? Would she really be able to do *that*? Wait, he told himself, hold your breath and see if the little roulette ball falls on the red or the black.

'You know what's bothering me?' she said with scornful familiarity. She sat down by the table. 'This stolen gun . . . If I kill him,I will owe you his death.' She shoved a few coins toward him, along with two or three bills pulled haphazardly from an envelope. 'Pay yourself,' she said, laughing. 'Render unto Caesar . . .'

Let's play along, he thought, picking up a ten-lira coin. 'If you insist, Marcella,' he said with a conciliatory professional gentleness meant to calm like a sedative. 'I

74

accept your money because when someone gives you a knife he asks for a coin; otherwise, the gift brings bad luck . . . Is that all you have left?'

'It's more than I need,' she said.

'Promise me something,' he said, to end the conversation. 'I won't try to dissuade you: the whole business would have to start again tomorrow, the day after tomorrow, or in a week. Go ahead if you want. Take that walk; go to the Balbo Palace—if you can get through the mob. Experiment with your resolution, or with your strength. I also have my own ideas on freedom . . . But if opportunity, courage, or faith fails you—believe me, there is no faith worth killing for, even less dying for— remember that somebody is there for you, in those ugly rooms, on the other side of the lighted balcony, among the throng and the footmen proffering drinks; someone only too happy *to applaud the action you will not carry out*. I'll go there too, on my own . . . After the speech, if nothing happens, I'll stand near the Corso, on the left side of the street, in front of the Mondo Theater.'

'Ready to escort me back?' she said, with a cutting laugh.

'Yes,' he said. 'For life.'

They were near the door. Passing by the room Massimo had gone into, he casually tried the door handle. If someone's in this room, he thought, it could only be the boy. In that case, what difference does it make?

'Remember that you condemned suicide,' he said in a voice unwittingly lower. 'This is suicide. You don't stand a chance.'

'My life is not worth more than that,' she said simply.

Only then did he realize that he did not know this Marcella he thought he knew. This project was more important to her than their love and their quarrels, and this fearlessness that put such a low price on life came from partisan despair and not from feminine anguish. Carlo's death has almost no part in it, he thought. And once again he felt a passionate curiosity that he would not have felt had he not loved her so much.

'I've been offered a position in England,' he said, trying a new tactic. 'If maybe . . .'

'No,' she said, pressing against him, though half unwillingly, because of the narrowness of the hall. 'All I ask of you is not to betray me.'

'Do you take me for your Russian student?' he said, raising his voice.

He picked up his hat. She was going to answer, but they were no longer alone. People were coming up the stairs. The door he had just opened let their chatter and laughter reach them. He said loudly: 'Tonight then, ten-thirty, in front of the Mondo Theater.'

She closed the door. As soon as he was outside, he became incredulous again. Cheap melodrama, he thought. She thought: 'I'll never see him again.'

She hesitated a moment before lighting the lamp. How tired I am, she thought. How slowly time passes . . . One more hour. Rather, two—especially if . . . She was parceling out her gestures and deliberately took the comb lying on the shelf above the sink, and ran it through her hair, noting with pleasure the steadiness of her hand. 'Alessandro,' she said aloud, mechanically repeating, out of habit, those syllables that already belonged to the past. She found the sponge and pressed it soaking wet on her face, chest, armpits, squeezing it as though the cold water also purified her blood and her heart. It would be better to change clothes, she thought, this broken strap . . . But her tiredness did not prevent her from listening to the silence and the imperceptible sounds in the next room. What does Alessandro think, she wondered. That . . . Could the boy still be there? . . . Impossible. But she felt burning shame, as if, instead of speaking with Alessandro, she had made love to him.

She knocked lightly on the wall. 'Are you there?'

'Yes.'

'Wait a second,' she said after a pause. 'I'll join you.'

Eavesdropping? She tried to think: it's disgusting, he's one of them. Alessandro's information is never wrong.

Or rather, no, she corrected herself, he was one of them. She did her best to feel the appropriate nausea, like a patient moving a numbed part of her body, unable to feel any sensation in it. So what, she thought. Massimo's presence filled the emptiness she had felt herself drifting into a moment earlier. It's like that intimacy with Carlo, she thought. I really thought so . . . I should have been indignant, I guess. No . . . Freed from conventions . . . After all, I'm entitled to spend my last hour with whomever I please, and she pushed the door open.

The room she entered was almost completely dark. Way in the back, a bare window provided a square of light from the street lamp and the shop windows; its harsh white mingled with the moonlight that was just beginning to emerge. The bed was in the dark area. Massimo lay on a bare mattress that smelled of mothballs; this banal funeral odor, smacking of the kind of straightening out that follows a departure, introduced a reference to Carlo's ghost into this stark room. Massimo raised himself, leaning on an elbow, like Hermaphroditus trying to leave his pedestal. He said softly: 'I heard everything.'

'You were spying on us?' she asked sadly.

'Yes . . . No . . . Let's say that I didn't want to leave without seeing you again.'

A moan answered him.

'Don't cry . . . Look, am I crying? . . . And don't blush either. First of all, because it's dark here . . . You love him,' he went on in a low voice, but he was so moved that he seemed to be screaming. 'You love *this man from another world*. In spite of yourself . . . You gave your secret to this insolent fool who is so sure of not being crazy like the rest of us, so sure of seeing the world as it really is . . . Oh, don't worry, he doesn't believe it. He was afraid for a moment, but he doesn't believe it . . .'

'Since I told him about it, I believe it a little less myself,' she interjected.

'But I believed it, I did, my Judith, I believe it since I

77

understood certain awkward questions about the firing range of weapons, and certain silences, and this air of being sure that you could today, all by yourself . . . You didn't tell me anything I didn't already know . . . And you yourself had guessed this black spot in my past, hadn't you? My past, what a ridiculous expression when one isn't even twenty-two yet . . . You don't pick up a stray dog without realizing that he is full of vermin.'

'Am I accusing you? Everything would have turned out the same without you.'

'It's hard, isn't it,' he said, suddenly thoughtful, 'the death of someone?'

'What's even harder is that he gave in before dying,' she said. 'But the point I'm at, it doesn't matter.'

'Hatred,' he went on in a singsong voice. 'Your hatred . . . When a man and woman insult each other the way you did a little while back, it's obvious they love each other . . . And did you hear her, this woman filled with hatred who loved Carlo? Your hatred . . . Oh, I know, it's not that you lack reasons: your father—strange that one can't talk of avenging a father without seeming to be part of an old melodrama—and Carlo, and the other one, the liberal who was bumped off on the banks of the Tiber—you know who I mean—and who is also unavenged. And in order to put an end to these lies scribbled in large letters on a wall . . . to shut this voice that throws this cheap mash to the crowds . . . But it's not true . . . You want to kill Caesar, but especially Alessandro, and me, and yourself . . . Cleanse the spot . . . Leave the nightmare behind . . . Shoot, as in a theater, to bring down the set behind the smoke . . . To be done with these people who are not real . . .'

'It's simpler than that,' said the weary voice. 'When I was a nurse in Bologna, I was always the one who did the dirty work no one else would do. Somebody has to do what others don't have the courage to.'

'. . . who are not real. Is he real, that one who beats on the fears of a class and the vanities of a nation as on a hollow drum? Are you real? . . . You are going to kill to try to feel real. And Carlo, who taught them, gave in, begged for mercy, then acted in such a way that mercy was no longer needed—was he real? We are all shreds of material, faded rags, a mixture of compromises ... The loved disciple is not the one asleep on the Master's shoulder in the paintings but the one who hanged himself with thirty pieces of silver in his pocket. Or rather, no: they are one man, one and the same man ... Like people who in dreams think they are someone else ... One dreams of killing or of being killed; one shoots, but shoots oneself. The noise of the explosion wakes one up: that's what death is like. Waking us up is death's way of reaching us ... Are you going to be awakened in an hour? Will you understand that killing is impossible, that dying is impossible?'

'How?' she asked, stifling a yawn. 'Suppose I miss him, they won't miss me.'

She heard him move restlessly on the bed.

'So you take your knife, Charlotte, and you climb into the coach for Paris, strike deep, like a butcher, right to the heart. Ah, killing, giving birth, you're all good at that, you women: at all the operations that involve blood ... And your sacrifice will save no one; on the contrary. Killing is only your way of dying ... Formerly'—and his voice stopped, then started up again quickly as if in delirium or under the influence of drugs—'long ago, some women, rebelling, went to the temples to break the idols; they would spit on them to make sure to be killed ... And public law and order was preserved, as you can well imagine: these women were wiped out, then chapels that looked like temples were built on their tombs ... This man, this false god, you won't kill him. Moreover, if he dies, he triumphs: his death is Caesar's apotheosis ... But you don't care ... This is the only way you can scream no when everyone is saying yes ... Ah, I love you,' he suddenly cried, 'I who would never have enough courage, or faith, or hope to do what you are doing, I love you ... Nemesis, my saint, my goddess, hatred that is our love, vengeance that is all we have of justice, let me kiss the hands that won't shake . . .'

He leaned over, lips half open, swept by an emotion both genuine and consciously exaggerated that was part of the actor and the visionary in him. She withdrew her hands, out of modesty or scorn, with a movement that grazed his face softly.

'Don't go off on a tangent to make me forget what I was thinking of. The letter?'

'What about it?'

'They showed it to you. You're still in contact with them?'

'Carlo knew it . . . Do you think you can escape that tangle so easily? . . . I protected you both more than you think.'

'You, too!' she said, with a quiet laugh.

A thin ray of moonlight, interrupted from time to time by the passing of clouds in the sky, was coming into the room. Massimo saw Marcella move, lift her arm.

'What are you doing?'

'I'm looking at the time. I don't want to go too early so that I have to wait in the piazza and be noticed. I still have time.' And, leaning back, she pressed her head against a corner of the pillow.

'Would you like to sleep? Want me to wake you?'

'No,' she said. 'I don't trust you that far.'

A minute passed; to both of them it seemed the equivalent of a long silence. Then, finally asking the question she had been dying to ask since she entered the room: 'Did you know about Carlo's death?'

'No,' he said in a low voice. 'I was expecting it, but I didn't know any more about it than you.'

'Do you think they killed him?'

'Who knows,' he answered in a muted tone. 'Enough . . . Leave it alone . . .'

'You see that I'm right to go tonight,' she said.

'No,' he said slowly, after thinking a moment. 'All in all, no . . . I want you to live.'

They held hands.

'Do you know what I'm thinking of,' she asked, almost

lightheartedly, deliberately speaking of something else. 'Of your complicated inventions. Of the false picture you painted with a little bit of truth . . . Alessandro . . . You . . . And Carlo himself thought . . . My father, for example. Yes, but I wasn't this heroic daughter Alessandro imagines . . . And Sandro . . . Yes, I loved him, and I missed him, and I fought against missing him. But sensual love is maybe not as important as one thinks . . .'

'Isn't that so,' he said eagerly.

I'm lying, she thought. Even so close to death, I'm lying. And nothing is simpler, since at the same time I love Sandro too . . . To think that I wouldn't dare look at this boy's face sometimes . . . What's he doing with this sick girl? If only I could be caressed by his hands, pull myself up a little on the pillow so that his head touches my breast . . . Too bad, that will never happen.

'It's for nothing,' he went on with bitterness. 'You're going there for nothing. They'll falsify everything, they'll turn everything to their advantage, even your attempted revenge. Tomorrow they'll say: a madwoman, crazy, the wife of a certain eminent doctor S—who . . . A little more mud thrown on Carlo . . . And me, they'll also use me to dirty your name.'

'And whose fault is that?' she said, withdrawing her hand.

They now spoke only from time to time, lazily, like travelers stretched out on benches in the waiting room of a train station who kill time until the train comes.

'A child,' he murmured almost reluctantly. 'A child who learned about hunger, war, escape, being arrested at the border . . . A child who saw everything but didn't suffer. For a child, it's a game. A student who misses classes, who takes money that he's offered here and there . . . Who goes on playing with life and death . . . A child one has inured to everything. "Like those who have no hope . . ." The day I got to know you, I understood. Perhaps you will change the world, since you changed me.'

'No,' she said. 'I haven't changed you. You are as you are.'

81

Breathing more quickly, he rose. In the half-light of the moon, his hair and face seemed made of the same pale and delicate matter. Marcella turned toward him a face that was also bathed in marble whiteness.

'Listen,' she said, putting her hand on his shoulder tenderly. 'A little while back, with Alessandro, I forgot everything for a moment. Everything: Carlo, and tonight's act. Several times . . . oh, only for a moment, but nevertheless . . . I am neither cleaner nor purer than you.'

'You know,' he went on in a low voice, 'sometimes I think that we're the ones who are not pure, we who have been humiliated, stripped, sullied, who without ever having lost anything have lost everything, who have no country, no political faith—no, no, don't protest—we could be the ones through whom the Kingdom will come. We are the ones who will no longer be corrupted, who cannot be deceived . . . Let's start right away . . . by ourselves . . . A world so different that it will make all the others fall, a world without noisy demonstrations, with no violence, especially without lies . . . But it will be a world where people will not kill.'

'You're like a child,' she said softly, making no pretense of listening to him, or hearing him. 'If I trust you, it's because you seem like a child.' She stretched, like a woman waking up. 'When I was living with Alessandro,' she said confidently, 'I wanted a child. A child by Sandro . . . Can you imagine: raised in a den for young Fascists . . . No, thank God . . . There are better ways of giving birth to the future.'

'The future,' he cried in an irritated voice, suddenly ironic. 'You've aggravated me enough, you and Carlo with your future generations, your future society, your future, your beautiful future . . . Your poor refuge for the persecuted . . . Look at the people in the street, later, when you go there, and ask yourself if they're the ones you build the future on. There is no future . . . There is only a man you want to kill, who, dead, will rise again like a target in a shooting gallery, a man who thinks he

82

can shape the future by banging his fists. Do you hear the voices answering him from the four corners of Europe, the voices howling hatred and predicting our future? And Carlo dead, dishonored, having perhaps ceased to believe in the future, and you with your pitiful short future . . . Or rather, no, I'm wrong,' he went on in a different tone, bending his head to read the time on his wrist turned toward the skimpy nocturnal light. 'Twenty to ten . . . You'll never be able to get through to the front row . . . It seems to me that you should put it off till tomorrow, your act that will change the future.'

'You think you're so clever,' she said. 'Do you think I would tell Alessandro the exact time, the exact place? I'm going to wait by the exit to the little piazza . . . There's a corner with a statue.'

'Playing a double game, you too,' he said tenderly.

She had gotten up, however, as if suddenly in a hurry to leave, in spite of herself.

'But in that case,' he said, also getting up, 'you still have a whole hour of sleeplessness to go through. Lie down again. You're tired,' he said with compassion.

'Don't insist,' she said. 'You did your best to make everything go wrong. You know that a person has only a limited amount of strength and that I've almost used up mine. But don't you feel that my whole life, even our moment of intimacy tonight, is grotesque if I don't do it? One would think that you envy my courage.'

'You don't have the courage not to do it. Would you like me to go in your place?'

'My poor boy!'

Tired of it all, he felt along the wall for the light switch, to try to give things back their banal appearance removed from danger and heroics. She stopped him.

'There is something else I'd like to know before going. Carlo never said anything about you . . . It's . . . It's like a betrayal on his part.'

'Ah!' he said in a lighter tone. 'These jealousies between disciples . . . How do I know? Leave those old stories alone. Since you don't want me to turn on the light,' he added, 'give me a cigarette. You know where they are.'

She went to bring them from the next room and gave them to him. Marcella's face appeared again in the tiny flame of the cigarette lighter; her face was no longer that of a marble statue but was human: a woman's face.

'My turn to ask a question,' he said. 'A little while back, that crazy woman . . . She sneered at you because of me.'

She blushed: he closed the lid of the cigarette lighter and with this gesture reestablished the darkness.

'You know better than anyone else that she was lying.'

'And what makes you think I don't regret it?'

'By saying that, you're really sending me out there,' she said.

She went back again into the kitchen. He heard her turn on the light, open and close a drawer, turn off the light. When she came back, she had a shawl over her head. They decided to leave by the Via Fosca. They walked through the shop together.

Suddenly, taking up an argument Alessandro had already used before him, he said: 'Carlo would not have approved of a crime.'

'What crime?' she asked, trying to understand. Then, 'Shut up!' she said with violence. 'What do you know about it.'

That's true, he thought, feeling cold anger. She knew him better than I did.

They opened the wooden blind very carefully, glancing down the deserted street stretching before them like a river of the night, contained by the dikes of houses; here and there, dim streetlights flickered like boat lanterns. This old street, by day invaded by the hustle and bustle of life, at night became stately again. But from some-where, through an open widow, came the incongruous whine of a popular song escaping from a radio. A few raindrops fell. Shivering in spite of the warm air, Marcella stopped; she felt like a swimmer about to dive.

How alone I am, she thought. And her hand on the door handle, she turned toward her uncertain companion. 'When I first came in, a little while ago, weren't you afraid . . . that I would start with you?'

'Not much,' he said. 'The point you're at, one doesn't waste one's bullets on small game.'

She closed the door. The fringes of her shawl caught in a chink of the blind; she pulled awkwardly, repressing a curse. He helped her get free.

All at once: 'Tell me goodbye,' she murmured. And she suddenly kissed him.

I'm kissing a dead woman, he thought.

That kiss, almost filial for him, almost incestuous for her, united them only for a moment in sad communion. Then, right away, they drew apart. The woman about to die remembered again with bitterness that she was ten years older than he. For a few more minutes, the proletarian heroine with the beautiful tragic face and the shady young customer of Viennese restaurants walked on, amicably holding hands.

Finally, as though waking from a dream: 'We mustn't be seen together,' she said. 'Where are you going?'

For a moment, he hesitated. She hoped that he would offer to follow her and she would have to prevent him from doing so. But, on the contrary: 'Nowhere, as usual.'

They separated. He did follow her, but at a distance, so that she did not notice; he had a dreamlike certitude that she would accomplish what she had set out to. She walked fast, gradually increasing the distance between them, proceeding with long, silent steps as if she were already a ghost. She emerged onto a big thoroughfare; here the crowd became denser, vain specters, empty bubbles, sticks of straw drawn into the vortex of an enormous voice. The river of shades widened, meandering along the dark façades in unexpected curves, carrying along in its waves inert, drowned corpses who thought they were alive. She was walking like a Greek woman in Hades, like a Christian one in Dante's Inferno, carrying a burden as old as History itself. Perhaps she passed, at

85

such and such a street corner, other prowlers, also isolated by their convictions or their hatred, who dreamed of witnessing or doing themselves what she sought to do tonight; but, to her, these people were ordinary strollers, as she was for them only an ordinary woman walking by. For the avenging gods do not recognize each other in their fleshly disguise. A burst of rain fell, making her thin summer dress cling to her body; she remembered with motherly concern that Massimo was very lightly dressed. But soon the image of the young man vanished from her memory; feeling more alone than ever, she kept on going, cleaving her way faster and faster through the night, blind and deaf to the storm that scattered the crowd. She remembered her father, then Carlo, as coldly as if they had both been buried for a long time; but now that she was going to act out her conviction, it became useless to be encumbered with these fidelities. There was no one at the entrance to the Mondo Theater, Alessandro was not there yet, or, more likely, no longer intended to wait for her. His house wasn't very far; maybe he was home; it was in her power to climb the stairs, ring the doorbell, and be admitted to that room, whose bed knew her body and whose mirror knew her shape. Instead of tugging at her heart, the image of this desire, already abandoned, deflected, floated into the distance and sank into oblivion. Freed from her flesh, she was only pure strength. The imminence of her act pushed back into the darkness the motives that had impelled her or that might still distract her from carrying it out; fatal, having become inevitable, it had a right to be absurd, like all things in life.

New bursts of rain stirred the darkness; the official festive lights wavered behind this curtain of water; flags at balconies luffed like sails in the wind. The showers falling on Piazza Balbo drowned out indiscriminately the last echoes of the speech, the clapping and cheering, and the silence that always follows. Marcella, standing at a corner of the Corso, took in the façade decked out with banners, the loggia from which the crowd, now dispersed by the riot of the elements, had been harangued by its god. She took in the car head-lights muted by mist; the cars were trying to move forward among the spattered pedestrians. She made a right turn at the corner and walked along the small Piazza Santo Giovanni Martire. Stooping, like a great nocturnal cat, she moved toward the church door at an angle to the palace, leaped onto the pedestal of the statue, and squeezed herself behind its bulk. Marcella stood in the narrow, dark space between the wall and the marble figure. There she was slightly above a group of drivers and policemen blinded by the rainstorm. The bad weather, disrupting the patrol, was in her favor. Rain bounced about her but did not touch her; tired, afraid only of firing too soon or too late, she mechanically tried to remember the name of the gun salesman who had repaired and oiled her weapon. Finally the door opened; a motor competed with the explosions of the storm. She had no trouble recognizing the man she had chosen as target among the small number of dignitaries nodding and smiling goodbye. But the moment she was living was different from what she had pictured. Instead of a ruler in uniform, chin lifted, facing and fascinating the crowd, she saw a man in evening clothes bending his head to climb into his car. She clung to the idea of the murder like a shipwrecked sailor hanging on to the only solid part of his sinking universe; she raised her arm, fired—and missed.

The usher's flashlight, like a burning eye, illuminated the floor of the loge. Angiola sat down, took off her long, suede gloves, letting them hang from her sides like two dead hands; she draped her coat on the back of the chair, then leaned forward on her elbows to watch Angiola Fides.

She had been able to slip away alone, right after dinner, from the drawing rooms of the Caesar Palace. Fortunately, Sir Julius Stein, filled with respect for his predecessors in the exploitation of the world, had just given to the past the first hours of his stay in Rome; his feet burning, his mind dazed by the pattern of the guide so that he now confused Julius Caesar with Pope Julius II, he had dragged himself through museums as though through the marble halls of an endless train station from where one could depart in all directions of Time. Furthermore, in spite of his admiration for the Great Man, the idea of a stroll in the city on a night of official speeches and public ceremonies did not appeal to him: one never knows how these things will end. Sunk in an easy chair, he was dozing now on the financial echoes of Wall Street or the London Stock Exchange, his own Capitol and his own Tarpeian Rock. The reporters still did not know of Angiola Fides's arrival: Angiola was therefore free tonight to give herself completely to the woman who made her heart beat. It was for Angiola that she had dressed, put on makeup, worn her pearls, and wrapped an unneeded fur around her neck; instead of prowling around Rome on foot as she had at first intended, she had taken a car to better enjoy the feeling of intimacy with this ghost. She had had herself driven to the portico of Santa Maria Minore, where Angiola Fides had formerly come to pray; she had gone down Via Fosca looking for the beloved, to offer her the necklace, the minks, the gold lamé shoes she wore only for Angiola. At every street corner, in front of posters displaying the scarlet pouting mouth of Angiola Fides, she had expected to find the little girl getting together enough pennies for the evening movie. She had even ventured as far as the courtyard of the wretched building her idol had lived in, but the crying, the shouting, the sordidness seeping from the slums at night, and especially the fear of running inopportunely into her possessive sister, had discouraged her from going up. She had settled for looking at the window against which, long ago, Angiola Fides would lean her uncombed street-urchin head and dream about all the things she did not have. Raindrops ran down Angiola's neck, drops as warm as the tears of a child not yet consoled. A fat, misshapen woman blocked the entrance and rudely asked the rich stranger what business she had in this house of poor people. Disconcerted, Angiola got back into the car, tossing the driver the address of a darkened room where she was sure to find Angiola Fides. Ignoring traffic regulations and outmaneuvering the throngs of people scurrying to escape the storm, the driver stopped on a quiet street, a few feet away from a brilliantly lit entrance plastered with posters of women: all beautiful, bigger than life, their shoulders bared provocatively. Angiola took a ticket from the cashier who serves as intermediary between us and the shadows, and sat down in a dark theater loge as in a room where she would have turned off the lights to be alone with someone.

The wall of the magic room came down: winds blew yet did not bring a breath of air into this cave full of specters, because they themselves were the ghosts of winds. The tunnel-like room opened suddenly on the

89

world. The dictator inaugurated a Roman art exhibition; Jews, guilty by virtue of their race, sneaked past the borders of the Reich; cannons thundered in the Mongolian desert. Closing her eyes, Angiola let those residual gestures, half digested by Time, pass by. For a few more weeks they would be scattered around the world, detached from their causes, before rotting like autumn leaves. She hadn't come to see these banal film shorts produced at great cost by the firm of God and Universe. Lapping laughter coursed through the amorphous crowd; a clown had just stumbled, trying to reach the object he thought he had at arm's length; after all, he was only doing what one does all one's life. Finally, her own voice came back to her like an echo bouncing off a white linen wall. Painted with light like the illuminated half of the globe, the huge face of Angiola Fides was bathed in a mist that seemed to come from her own breath. The face turned slowly toward night; the temples and forehead were bordered by a dark forest, the cheeks were valleys under delicately protruding bones, the eyes were deep lakes, the lips opened to reveal the interior abyss. She ran her fingers through her hair to pull back a strand from Angiola Fides's forehead, forgetting she had changed hairstyles. In a way, she was watching a dead woman. The magic room, crude reproduction of human memory, could only bring her back as she no longer was. Also, in a sense less stupid than the literal, she was facing a vampire: this pale monster had drunk Angiola's blood yet had not succeeded in becoming flesh. She had sacrificed everything to this ubiquitous ghost whom the camera granted a factitious immortality, not immune, however, from death. She had exploited her sorrows so that Angiola Fides could learn to cry, so that her smile might be tinged with scorn. As an adolescent, she had filled her dreams with images of this Angiola, happier, more perfect than herself. In an illusion shared by lovers, who think they can be one with the object they love, she thought she would feel identified with her idol. When she died, she would try to imitate one of Angiola's deaths. But this ghost was a rival. She got nothing, or almost nothing, out of these desires aroused in the dark by this *femme fatale* who could not live in sunlight. Like Narcissus at the edge of luminous waves, she looked for herself in Angiola Fides's reflection, in vain.

She sang: the enormous mouth opened, resembling a classical mask pouring out floods of tragedy. A spectator applauded, unable to believe in the deafness of this eloquent face. Angiola unconsciously hummed the song Angiola Fides belted out at the top of her lungs. She smiled, fascinated by her own self; her smile was but a faint carbon copy of the untouchable idol's. A flute trilled sharply like the tongue of a reptile: she danced. Angiola herself was only the body of this gigantic shadow projected on the white wall of the world. Sitting still, she watched the shadow of her muscles, the shadow of her bones, the shadow of her flesh.

Alternately rising and sinking in the dark, a flash of shoulders and of half-naked hips appeared, then disappeared in the empty rectangle. Caught by this slow shuddering of a snake in mating season, Angiola undulated in the back of the loge from hips to shoulders, imperceptibly, like an Eve joined to her snake.

It was an island under palm trees, at the edge of a Mediterranean that recalled the Pacific. One recognized the sound of the waves but not their color: sunlight effects were changed into moonlight effects. Algenib, or rather, Angiola Fides, because no role could disguise her real personality, any more than any piece of clothing could keep her from being naked, was picking one-dimensional pomegranates in the garden; their juice would darken no kitchen knife: they were pomegranates for ghosts. Algenib's father had drowned himself, leaving his daughter in the care of a Moorish woman with a heart of gold. In reality, Don Ruggero might still be vegetating in his asylum and the dull Rosalia, who loved her sister so much that she taught her to love only herself, probably still lived in three rooms and a kitchen

91

on the top floor of the Via Fosca building; but Angiola was not the kind to be encumbered by a family who would disturb the embellished picture she presented of her past.

Algenib and an English officer exchanged a kiss on their first meeting, under flowering hibiscus. Angiola's first lover was not English and wore no uniform: he was a tailor from Palermo who had invited her to look at his samples, and because the back of the shop was not completely dark, Angiola remembered, she was ashamed as she undressed, since there were holes in her stockings. Grief-stricken because Lord Southsea had left, Algenib threw herself at the feet of the Madonna, in a chapel full of nuns delicately made up. Angiola had been forced to go to a boarding school in Florence where she hated the gray-faced nuns. This racy but moral movie, produced to pass all the censors of the world, did not mention the many strangers the adolescent Algenib had been as accommodating to as Angiola, during her escapades, in the San Miniato gardens or on Piazza Addaura. But Angiola herself had put aside such memories. A French painter wearing a romantic felt hat tenderly wiped Algenib's dazzling and pearly tears; they had met on a pink back-lit beach. Angiola would willingly have been faithful to this great artist of exquisite tact and experience with women; unfortunately, at an age when one is still capable of gratitude, luck had put a Paolo Farina in her path; he had been foolish enough to marry her after the little Marquis of Trapani, out of cowardice, had dropped her. Algenib left her generous but impoverished protector for a maharaja with flashy teeth; a sworn enemy of the British, he involved her in his spying activities. Angiola had run away from the conjugal nest with a tenor with gold-filled teeth. Algenib shot the Chief of British Intelligence in a bar in London. Angiola had handled her share of daggers and Brownings, but whereas Algenib had had to deal with inconstant lovers and traitors, Angiola had confronted only actors. Disguised as an Indian dancing girl, Algenib fell prostrate before Shiva, showing off the curvy hip of Angiola Fides. During a reception at the Residence, Algenib quietly slunk into the office of a British commander to steal a secret document. The door opened; the draft from an electric fan scattered the state documents. Lord Southsea's Greek profile and flashlight appeared in the darkness. Algenib turned, feeling the stranger's hand on her shoulder . . .

Not long after Angiola's arrival, a man had come into the loge; in the usher's light, she caught a glimpse of a white shirtfront and a handsome, slightly worn face that by comparison seemed gray. He had come in to find shelter from the storm: no point thinking of a taxi on such a night, in the rain and with this crowd. The presence of another person irritated him, broke into his solitude. He sat as far away as possible; that is, still too close. But it wasn't the rain that kept him from going home. After leaving Marcella, he had had himself driven immediately to the Balbo Palace. Certain, in spite of himself, that something would happen, he had quickly crossed the gilded reception rooms filled with uniforms and evening clothes. Stationed by the entrance, ready to defend the woman though he did not approve of her—in fact, disapproving—just as a skeptic indifferent to any god might, out of love, join a Christian woman thrown to the beasts, he had absurdly sought to identify her head among the anonymous many. From bombastic sentence to bombastic sentence, from raised fist to raised fist, under a sky more and more threatening, in the sweating enthusiasm of the crowd, he had in turn dreaded, hoped, despaired that a shot would ring out. The speech, longer than usual, had ended under cheers dampened by the storm. Crossing the street with the throng fleeing the rain, he duly kept the appointment at the entrance of the Mondo Theater. But after a while he gave up his ridiculous watch. It was highly unlikely that Marcella would come, willing to parade her defeat. She probably went home and threw herself on the bed, to cry or sleep.

It occurred to him that such a humiliation might bring a woman back to reality, to love; he might well find her at his house, waiting on his front step, insipid as failure, reduced by the admission of her cowardice to be for him now only a lover like other women; the repulsion he felt at this idea made him realize that what he loved in her was in fact the courage she obviously lacked.

The usher closed the door and darkness reigned once more. A small red lamp on the wall recalled the lamp hanging over Marcella's bed. To shut it off, he closed his eyes. In order to punish himself, he went over the incidents that had turned his evening into a grotesque nightmare, and thought it fitting that the rain had chased him under this marquee, then into this room that at least was dark. Perhaps Marcella had only invented her project, to mystify him while getting rid of him: he pictured her sitting on her bed, near Massimo, under the Virgin of Loreto transformed doubtless into a kind of icon by the young Russian, both of them laughing at his gullibility; then he pushed back that image, not because it was false, but because he could not bear it.

He opened his eyes: acclamations were echoing like thunder in his memory; his hands clenched at this repetition of his nightmare; the film of his life was running backwards: flags waved back and forth against a stone façade: a thickset character was fishing enthusiasms in the plankton of crowds; sitting on the edge of his seat, Alessandro once again expected the punctuation of a gunshot after each sentence, then suddenly remembered that one doesn't shoot ghosts. It wasn't the present he had just lived through, it was a newsreel, events one week old. This public of opium smokers, mouths open as though sucking on their dreams, chewed over again, before falling asleep, the events of the week like shreds of reality still rising at night on the edge of sleep. Hypnogenetic hallucinations began in the guise of cartoons: incongruous characters, lighter than men, multiplied and chased one another like the fear, the enthusiasm, the indignation and irony Alessandro had experienced

during his pathetic waiting. The high waters of the
dream invaded the room, dragging drifting memories
and symbolic fauna with them. A clown fell, stumbling
against emptiness like Alessandro against an absent
woman. The heroine shot her enemy dead: the blood
flowing was hemoglobin. The only difference between
this movie and life was that here the public knew it was
being deceived. There were no tyrants since there were
no rebels, there were no beings but a sequence of dis-
sociated characters with jerking gestures soldered
together by speed to give the illusion that they existed.
The whole thing was nothing but two-dimensional
deception, hollow declamation on a sonorous surface. A
woman danced, false, since she was impalpable: a useless Venus emerging from the undulations of the waves.
Half naked also, but very close, warm, touchable, faintly
lit from the inside by the secret sun of blood, the living
shoulder of a young woman blocking part of the screen
was the only protecting wall between Alessandro Sarte
and all these ghosts. Unwittingly imitating the boldness
of the actor, thereby becoming his opaque double, he put
his hand lightly on the delicate rock of flesh; his gesture
was less a voluptuary's than a castaway's.

The shoulder bathed in night shook softly like a reef
seeming to follow the movement of waves. It stopped
trembling suddenly, as if, once touched, the woman was
pretending to be insensible. Stiff but consenting,
Angiola stayed in character by yielding to the desire her
shadow flesh had awakened. With this stranger
reaching for Angiola Fides, she had the sensation that
she was supplanting a rival. With this anonymous
woman, he was taking revenge on an absent one. Feeling
for the sensitive zones along her body, he was once
again struck by the resemblance between the gestures
of love and medical gestures: the yielding of this woman,
gradually subjugated by pleasure, was not unlike the
involuntary start, the spasms or the docility of a patient.
He dismissed this idea which spoiled his pleasure, and,
in order to increase it, concentrated entirely on her

hand moving imperceptibly like a marine plant. Like a mirror on a bedroom ceiling, the screen sent them back the indistinct image of a couple: the enlarged reflection was of a gigantic kiss, blown open like a flower, suggesting, on the narrow space of lips and eyelids, the embrace of the whole body. Had the image been any larger, the faces would have disintegrated into moving atoms as indifferent to that kiss as we may be to the unbounded loves of stars. Head thrown back, eyes closed, Angiola saw colors dancing behind her lids. Algenib recognized Lord Southsea: hunted by the British police, the lovers reached the edge of the sea. The pirogue sank on a Pacific that looked like the Mediterranean; the fugitives died together. The great pleasure wave was spent, rose again, bringing the two drowned lovers to the surface. Angiola huddled closer to the man, who was already withdrawing from her; Alessandro moved back, caught by a thought as he came out of his moment of oblivion. This stupid scenario expressed what had been for an instant his absurd secret desire: he also, a little while ago, had wished to join Marcella in the culmination of death. The image of calmed waters spread over the screen being slowly swallowed by a wave of darkness. Then the light came on abruptly, a yellow light well suited to the hustle and bustle of the living. He saw now, standing before him, only a heavily made-up woman who was looking at herself in her pocket mirror before leaving.

Before she opened her mouth, her rather abrupt gestures, and the cut of her clothes, made him identify her as a foreigner, an American perhaps, one of these travelers who go through love as if visiting cities. Like all women striving for a Hollywood face and soul, she did her best to look like Angiola Fides. But her handsome features were infinitely less expressive than those of the startling actress who had just filled the screen. An Angiola Fides able to mimic passion so well must also have been able to feel and inspire it. On the other hand, this easy conquest was the type of woman one did not get saddled with.

Despising her, and at the same time grateful to be able to despise all women in her, he nevertheless respected the pleasure she had just dispensed. Movie English was for him, as it was for many men of his generation, one of the secret slangs of love. He ventured: 'Thank you, my love. It was wonderful.'

'My dear man,' she answered slowly in English while putting on lipstick, 'don't think I do that with everybody.'

The predictable nonsensical lie irritated him. Another woman who pretends to find in each man, if not her first lover, at least her first love.

'I don't expect excuses,' he said curtly.

Not answering, she swallowed hard, in a small movement that made her seem pathetic. Another man, she thought, who because of ten minutes of intimacy feels authorized to be insolent, crude, or clingingly tender. It was better not to get involved with strangers, who tomorrow might try to inveigle her into some shady business deal, or might send anonymous letters to Sir Julius. It's only in movies that lovers yield, with no ulterior motives, to passions meant to last a lifetime; that is, till the end of the film. This ordinary man was less real than Lord Southsea.

'A stupid movie, wasn't it?' she said.

'Yes,' he answered with bitterness. 'Stupid as life itself.'

English put a barrier between them which neither sought to cross. He did not notice that she spoke it as badly as he did.

'American?'

She nodded. It wasn't a big lie. British soon, if she could have her ridiculous marriage annulled and marry Sir Julius, who, however, is Australian. Money, or rather the printed paper that today passes for money; the prestige of a title as recent as her shadow-theater-actress fame—all this glitter for Sunday newspaper readers, what more could a woman get who can only ape life? Angiola can't enjoy the great emotions she is so good at arousing in others: in real life, her loves are aborted, one after the other, like her only child. In Palermo, for her first love, she simulated cynicism; with Tonio di Trapani, she played the innocent. Still pale from loss of blood when Paolo Farina proposed marriage, she pretended to be repentant. Leaving him for her small-town opera singer, she thought she was doing the right thing by mimicking remorse. In Tripoli, with Sir Julius Stein, the AFA backer, Angiola, in reality a hooker who got a walk-on part, pretended to be a woman in distress. Here, with this newcomer, she would have been capable only of mimicking love.

'Italian.'

'Passing through Rome.'

Lie, cut yourself off from the others, plunge deep into deceit as into the interior of an island. What is a woman? Is he going to be trapped by two eyes pretending to be sad? This room, half empty already and bathed in electric light, no longer holds the images of his frenzy. After all, she told herself, looking at him, he's not bad; I could do worse. Still, it's better that he should not guess who I am.

'Sometime soon again?' he asked unconvincingly.

'Impossible.'

He does not insist. Each, for his part, now wants to be alone. She slips the little heart-shaped mirror in her purse. He helps her with her coat: the silk edged with fur makes him think, with some tenderness, of the secret of her body. Exorcised, the public is hurrying for the exit. He feels less detached than usual from these people who came here to satisfy their taste for romance and tragedy. Angiola wonders how many of them will see her in their dreams tonight. As he walks with this woman, he notices with some pride that people turn to look at her, or at least at her pearls.

'Shall I get you a taxi?'

'I have a car.'

The rain has stopped. The driver is waiting on a side street. She has to stoop to get in. Through the lowered windows, Alessandro sees only a smile just melancholy

98

enough, and two slim hands slipping on gloves; she is a lover interchangeable with any other. If Marcella comes back to him tonight (reason tells him that nothing of the sort will happen), he will be angry at himself for having offered stupidly to disrupt his life for an unhinged woman, a liar who thought she had hoodwinked him. His imagination evokes a more realistic picture of the empty apartment, the easy chair he will sink into, letter opener in hand, to read a review or a medical journal; he will stop after every sentence to berate himself for his ridiculous gullibility. He's going to try to go home as late as possible.

'Beautiful roses . . . Beautiful carnations . . . Beautiful roses . . .'

'Wait,' he tells the driver.

As he drops the price of the roses in the old woman's scraggy hand, half a dozen lictors dressed in dark shirts are taking up the width of the sidewalk with their excited movements. A sentence caught by chance triggers something in him, all the more disturbing because he had perhaps unconsciously still been expecting it. Letting the car with the woman and the roses drive off, he walks up to a bodyguard who seems to be quite agitated and whom he recognized as a friend.

'You here? . . . Do you know what happened?'

The soft face of the fat man seems ravaged by the storm. Alessandro has time to put a mask of surprise on his own face. Repressed possibilities rise to the surface of his anxiety. Arrest? Carrying illegal weapons? He pictures the telephone ringing nonstop by his bedside in his empty room. Is he compromised? Alessandro ran out of heroic inclinations a few hours ago. The whole business is now only an idiotic venture to him.

'. . . Out of her mind . . . Your family name . . . Maria . . . (How the hell should I know . . .) Marcella Sarte . . . No, no: she didn't say anything . . . She didn't stop firing until . . . Her ID papers . . . found on her . . . my poor man, what a mess . . .'

The chatter of his kind friend prevents Alessandro's self-control from dissolving into nightmare. She really dared to do it? Since Marcella will never know, Alessandro deems it pointless to admit he admires her, and he would probably not understand himself if he admitted that right now he envies her. Alongside this ordinary fellow, he acts the way anyone else would have in his place.

The two men head, almost running, for the nearest police station. Inside, where a pitiless white light flows uninterruptedly from an electric bulb like the cold water flowing from a faucet of the morgue, two forms are laid out next to each other. A young boy from a paramilitary group was senselessly struck by one of the five bullets fired haphazardly into the night; his head, emptied by a wound, hangs to one side. His childish face has been dutifully covered up with the cape of a uniform; the hard smoothness of marble has already overcome his features. Next to him on the tile floor has been placed a woman beaten to death; the morning newspapers will call her, with scornful condescension, a deranged person. These two victims of different gods are counterbalanced in death. A black dress soaked with rain clings to the body of the murderess, giving the corpse the appearance of drowning. A little bit of blood and saliva has dribbled from the gaping mouth, but the face is intact. A damp strand of hair snakes along the cheek of this dead Medusa. And her eyes, wide open but blind, contemplate the void which is now her whole future.

Old Mother Dida sat down under a portico again, between her two baskets still half filled with unsold flowers wilting in the heavy storm weather. She pulled her kerchief over her hair, which, if washed, would be white; tucked her feet under her as protection from the puddles, and raised her fist to the thunder.

When young, Mother Dida had looked like a flower; now she looked like a tree trunk. She was hard of hearing; her big gnarled hands seemed to protrude from her like branches; her feet, slow to lift, stuck to the ground as if rooted. Her dead children rotted in the cemetery like autumn leaves; even her gods were themselves like some sort of enormous flowers. Little bud Jesus was born at Christmas, fresh and fragile as a primrose; at Easter time, already full grown, letting his bearded head crowned with thorns hang like fruit, he expired on the tree of the Cross. This was the proof that he was God; no one lives thirty years in the space of twelve weeks. The other proof that he was God was that Mary made him all by herself: if Dida had been told that about the mother of an ordinary man, she would not have believed it. Some Jesuses were richer than others; a few knew how to read, like the Bambino of Aracoeli, to whom the poor wrote when they were in trouble. Sometimes these Jesuses were nice, they listened to you; then they would grow deaf or angry and no one knew why. It's like the sun baking up things when people wanted rain, or hiding when one really needed a blue sky. Then there was the wind, which now is here, now is not, because the whole world is nothing but a big whim; and the moon showing whatever face she wants, and the fire catching because that's why there's fire. There is also the government, always saying that you owe it money, and having people killed in times of war, but that's the way it is because that's the way it is; there have to be strong people to lead and rich ones to make poor people work. Then there was also the dictator, who wasn't there before but the King named him to run things for him. He's good for the country but he's hard on those who are against him (the Belotti boy was handcuffed, how sad), but he's right because he's the strongest. And then there was Rome, where Old Mother Dida had been selling flowers for thirty-five years, and from one end of the world to the other, you couldn't find a bigger or more beautiful city than Rome, and that's why so many foreigners come here. And on the other side of Rome, on the side that wasn't Ponte Porzio's, there was the sea, which Dida had never seen but her son Nanni had crossed to go to Argentina, and Attilia's children sometimes went to the sea by bus, on Sundays, on holidays. And all around Rome there was bad land, all you could grow on it was grass for sheep, but also there were roads with trucks and dust, because that's progress; and every year more and more factories and tourist sites with restaurants where people who are well off go. And, here and there, you could see vegetable gardens, and fields where flowers were grown in tight rows, to be sold in Rome, and greenhouses glittering in the sun like the ones her son, Ilario, was taking care of right now. Then, much farther, on the side where there was Florence and where her daughter, Agnese, lived with her husband, who was a coachman, there were mountains where in winter you could see snow. And as far as you went, in all directions, it was like that with the land under the sky. And in the middle of all these things, which became clearer the closer they were to her, was herself, Mother Dida of Ponte Porzio.

When she was asked when and where she was born,

Dida answered that it was in Bagnani, on the Anio, a long time ago, even before the King came to Rome. She had had so many brothers and sisters that she couldn't keep their names straight in her head. Her mother had soon died, and Dida had to take her place and take care of all God's little lambs, but, fortunately, when the Lord gives a lamb He also provides the grass: vineyards were good business in those days. Then, strange as it may seem, she had been a handsome girl with breasts round as love apples under her shirt. She had married Fruttuoso, the former gardener of Villa Cervara, who quit because he had a falling-out with the landlords: a piece of land at Ponte Porzio was bought to raise flowers on. When it came to sowing, bedding plants, pruning, clipping, Fruttuoso knew more about it than anybody else. Children had come, maybe eight, maybe nine, counting those who were born premature and those who lived only a few days, but those, they were little angels. Once again, all those little lambs of God had to be raised; you had to wash them, feed them, smack them to teach them manners, teach them to earn their bread at the age of nine when they left school. At the crack of dawn, Fruttuoso went to Rome in his painted wagon to do the selling; he would come back, early morning, half asleep, through flat and pink roads; his little horse knew the way. One day, at a level train crossing, the express threw itself like a wolf on the man and harness, crushing their cattle-bell sound. The little horse was sent to the knacker, and Fruttuoso to the cemetery, where he slept under a wreath made of brass wire, which lasted longer but was just as nice as real flowers.

Dida ran into hard times, which in her memory were mixed with the hard times of World War I, when her eldest son was killed in Caporetto. Even though the children were big enough to help their mother, she hired a man to do the heavy work; after ten months, they had another christening: he wasn't a bad man, this Luca, but he was more of an expert in women than in flowers. The children were growing up: Dida, becoming stingier and less amorous with age, grew tired of feeding this bare-foot tramp who had once let all her roses die, out of laziness; but she was scared to fire him, scared of the sharpness of his knife. At last, her three sons beat the idea of leaving into Luca's head. A howling Dida accompanied her Luca to the turn of the road; he was covered with bandages, and was screaming threats; her face was streaming with tears; she cursed her sons, the dogs, who were so cruel to their poor mother; she couldn't even afford to give him a new cap and jacket as a goodbye gift; her heart bled to see him leave. He knew she was lying; she knew he wasn't fooled: for a few nights afterwards, the family stayed up, afraid Luca might come back and set fire to the place or ransack the greenhouse, but instead he took revenge by finding another widow to hire him.

Then it was the children's turn to be refused things by Old Mother Dida, this one some tobacco and shiny shoes for dancing on Sundays, that one some ribbon, some pomade, or a piece of silk. Nanni was carried off, like his father, by the express: he took the train for Naples and the liner for Buenos Aires. Agnese, who had left to become a lady's maid in Florence, set up house with a coachman, who was a good man, but their little one turned out badly; she hadn't written in ten years or sent a money order. Attilia had married this good-for-nothing Marinunzi. But Ilario, now that one was serious: he knew that flowers were money. And the two other daughters were not afraid of work; the youngest, Luca's, wasn't quite right in the head, but she worked the hardest. Scarecrows in their man's shoes, faded smocks, skin sallow and wrinkled like an old woman's, they rise before dawn to bundle up the merchandise, toil all day, get up again to put straw mats over the flowers or feed the stoves: no danger here that a lover will come and carry them away, snatch them from Old Mother Dida. As for Ilario, Dida had advised him against taking a wife; there were enough people to take care of the greenhouse, and girls today were worthless when it came to housekeeping. They had sold a piece of land for development, for Ponte Porzio was no longer all country; the greenhouse had been enlarged on the land that was left. Ilario's customers were big florists on Via Veneto; Dida didn't really have to go to Rome every day to sell flowers, as she had been doing since the time of her second widowhood.

But Rome had become a habit with her; she liked being dropped off by Ilario's small truck on the marble steps of the entrance to the Conti Palace, between the movie theater that had been there on the left for ten years (it was good for business) and the Café Imperio on the right on an adjoining street; the woman who owned the café let Dida leave her unsold flowers overnight in pails in the back corridor. Dida liked noise, and here she had plenty of noise; she liked the neighborhood and felt as important as the princess who lived on the first floor of the palace, who bargained for flowers every morning. In the thirty years she had been working on these steps she had seen many things change; the big white building there, at the back of the piazza, had grown before her very eyes; she had outlived a King and three Holy Fathers. She liked her trade: she smiled at people knowingly to make them think she remembered them; she learned to spot foreigners, aware that they seldom asked for their change because it was too complicated, and besides they're rich, all of them. She knew who bought flowers to take to the hospital or to the cemetery, or to relatives, or especially on the feast days of Santa Maria or San Giovanni, for a girlfriend, or for pleasure because the weather was nice, or, on the contrary, because the weather was gloomy, or sometimes even out of a love of flowers. She liked the little café where at noon she drank her espresso; they let her bring her own odorous lunch wrapped in newspaper. She liked going home on the last bus, treated with respect by the conductor. She walked the few hundred yards of rural road to her house, with its eternally closed shutters, hurrying, afraid of being attacked. Then, while a tousled

Tullia or Maria came down to heat her plate of pasta, you could hear her drag her chair across the tile floor of the kitchen as she fumed at this hovel that was fit only for animals, cursing her lazy children, who didn't work nearly as hard as she did.

She had the reputation of being mean: she was hard as the earth, eager like a root seeking sustenance, choking weaker roots in her shadow, stormy and sly as water. To generations of plant creatures, she had been the Good Mother and ruthless Fate, but all those anemones, peonies, and roses had only been raw material to her, things born of soil and fertilizer, grown and cut to earn a living. She had always exploited her men in pleasure and in work; they had been her tools. She had groaned and moaned for her departed and her dead, then forgot them the way animals forget vanished stable companions or their young ones taken from them. As for the children who were left, she had trained them to bring her their earnings like dogs retrieving quail. She stuck money in hiding places out of reach of Attilia's greediness and her good-for-nothing husband; even Ilario, out of respect, pretended not to know their exact location. But the best hiding place was the filthy pouch she wore around her neck; it contained, like Sacred Hosts, the family's bank notes carefully folded. It was her scapular, her Jesus, her God, who would always provide for her. Because of this money, one of these days her son-in-law Marinunzi would cut her throat, or one night on the road Luca would do her in, or even Ilario, who had been seen prowling around with a rope, would strangle her, incited by some nasty, unscrupulous woman; and Dida dreamed of murderers like an old tree dreaming of the woodcutter.

'Dida, you'll go to hell,' said Father Cicca, priest of Santa Maria Minore, that morning. He had stopped before the well-stocked baskets and was glancing sidelong at the roses, which he would have liked for the chapel of Our Lady of the Immaculate Conception.

Without answering, Dida went on breaking off pieces of straw between her teeth; she used those pieces as string to tie the flowers.

'You'll go to hell,' he went on, 'and the proof is that you're already there. You will be resurrected on Judgment Day with your fist clenched, like all misers, and you will spend eternity trying in vain to open your hand. Just think about it, Dida, your hand in an eternal cramp! You've never let drop a coin for a mass for your dear departed; you're hard with yourself and mean with others; you've never thrown a bone to a dog. One nice gesture for once, Dida, give me some roses for the Holy Virgin.'

'Damn you,' grumbled Old Mother Dida. 'Your Virgin is richer than I am.'

But her old face stopped frowning and smiled at good Father Cicca, who came from the same village and thirty years before had found her this good spot right next to Santa Maria Minore. She would gladly have given him something for his Holy Virgin if she had the means. But she never had the means, and the priest, not too disappointed, went off; his shoes were too big for his feet, his soiled cassock dragged along the ground, and he was pulling his grumpy friend, the blind organist, by the arm. The two men squabbled constantly yet never left each other's side; Santa Maria Minore was a haven for the blind man, and he in turn was a treasure for Father Cicca. Moreover, they loved each other dearly; habit had long made brothers of them. Their lot in life was similar: well-intentioned people had had the blind man learn music, because you don't need eyes for that; and Father Cicca had been ordained because pious persons had offered his needy family to pay for his schooling. But it so happened that the blind man was gifted in music and that Father Cicca loved God. Like all human happiness, their happiness was precarious and imperfect: the organist suffered from the icy cold in church in the winter and was hurt, in all four seasons, that he had not been invited to play at the music school of St. Cecilia,

107

which was famous: even music had its moments of emptiness and disgust when Bach was nothing but complicated noise; then, all at once, this mediocre musician would be lifted to the heavens on the wings of a fugue. Father Cicca had his problems with the bishop, with his needy family, who were a constant burden; and he had cravings, childish but as violent as those of a profligate, for things he would never have: a beautiful gold watch, a new, electric chandelier for his church, a shiny, noisy little car like the ones seen in great numbers on the streets of Rome. But at night, on his hard bed, the old priest would suddenly wake up filled with joy and murmur 'God . . . God . . .' as if dazed by an ever-new discovery granted only to him to make, which he couldn't communicate to his flock—not to Dida, who loved only money; not to Rosalia di Credo, who didn't know God is everywhere and not just in Sicily; not to the Princess of Trapani, whose worry was her son's debts. 'God . . .' he would murmur. 'God . . .' He sighed, ashamed of owning God like a privilege, like a possession he couldn't share with others, which he hadn't earned any more than they. And just like Dida's money, which was coveted by evildoers, the organist's heaven was threatened by deafness, and the old priest's was spoiled by scruples.

It was still thundering; Dida lowered her head, worried about the lightning's striking haphazardly as if no one were innocent. Luckily, however, the storm had crossed to the side of the sea; it was no longer raining in Rome, or on the fields of Ponte Porzio. But the day, with its showers since afternoon, had been bad for business. And those political speeches, you've got to have some, but that's not what sells flowers. Since nine o'clock that night, Dida had seen thousands of backs of people turned to a spot on the piazza that could not be seen from her corner. The shouts and the clapping had reached her as a great undefined noise. Then the burst of rain and the surge of the crowd had forced her to seek shelter in the entryway of the café, and when finally the street had regained its usual nightly aspect, the last bus for Ponte Porzio had long since left the station square. It's true, she could spend the night in Trastevere with Attilia, who was expecting her fourth, but that was some distance away and she preferred not to be indebted to that scoundrel Marinunzi. The simplest thing was to stay where she was and wait for the early-morning arrival of Ilario's truck; she could always spend what was left of the night in the courtyard of the Conti Palace, where the janitor knew her.

But first it would be a good idea, before the Café Imperio closed, to use the toilet at the end of the passage, which was something the owner let her do. This bathroom was for Dida one of the chief advantages of her spot. The place had a particular charm one felt even as one approached the door, which was all mirror; it now reflected a woman who, Dida knew, would have made heads turn thirty years ago. One was very comfortable sitting, skirts lifted, in this place lit by electricity, protected from air and wind. The sound of water running nonstop because of an old leak was a sound of luxury one would not have heard in Ponte Porzio, where there was plumbing for the flowers but no running water for the house. But you had to be careful to leave everything very clean, especially since so many foreigners came here.

Just as Dida was coming back out, the owner of the café was closing up the passageway. Under her slick hairdo, the woman was very pale. 'What a terrible evening, Dida. Somebody tried to shoot *him*, at the exit . . . A client told me . . .'

'You're right, this is not normal weather for this time of year,' said Dida, knowing that when people address you they nearly always talk about the weather.

'What! I'm telling you someone tried to shoot *him* as *he* was leaving,' the woman shouted at the top of her lungs. She wanted to enjoy the excitement, the indignation, the news . . . 'The client saw the mark of the bullet on the car window . . . It just missed! . . . It was a woman, imagine that ... and young, it seems ... Another attempt by these know-nothing anarchists, socialists, communists, who knows what—all these people who get money from abroad ... We've been too soft on them, Mother Dida. And the woman? She's dead, of course. One had to ... she fought, she clung on ... Some say they were grenades, not bullets ... There's blood on the ground at the entrance to Santo Giovanni Martire ... a puddle of blood ... Good night, Dida, I'm sure I won't sleep a wink ...'

Slowly, uncertainly, Dida goes back to sit on the steps for a moment, leaning against the closed door, among the bouquets, which she forgot to put in water. She is afraid, so afraid that she doesn't dare get up and leave, turn her back on this piazza now completely dark. And she is alone ... The owner just left, not even noting that at this late hour Dida has no bus to take, but there are other things on her mind besides Dida, naturally. What an awful night. It's not a world for Christians, she says to herself; even animals would know better ... Someone tried to kill him, the one the King gave the right to lead. And that's a crime ... Nothing can be right in such a world anymore. Things are worse than when the King was killed, the year poor Fruttuoso died. And that woman ... In spite of herself, Dida felt a twinge in her heart at the thought of her. A puddle of blood ... She must have had courage to do a thing like that. Maybe they did something to her ... Furtively, embarrassed as though she were being watched, Dida made the sign of the cross for the dead woman; it didn't cost anything, and one day it might help if someone did as much for her, with a little prayer.

Dida presses herself further against the door. So close, only a few feet away, on the other side of the empty piazza, where there's only the usual policemen now, patrolling two by two ... Yes, but they probably sprinkled the blood with sand. Yet Death had passed by there; it didn't take him, but it took the woman; perhaps it was still roaming around, looking for someone else.

110

When the time comes, there's nothing you can do. And what had come over the damn priest this morning, saying she'd be resurrected fist clenched? Dida, who did not know that Father Cicca was paraphrasing Dante, moves her knotty fingers slowly, but in fact they never open completely. So what? She isn't stingy, she's only poor. As for money, you have to save it, or you'll be a burden to others when something goes wrong. It's true that she was hard on her children, but that was to discourage the lazybones from falling into bad ways; Father Cicca didn't have a right to call her heartless. What he doesn't know, luckily, is that yesterday when she came home she found old Luca drinking in her kitchen, whimpering with joy in his glass. With Tullia and Maria's help, she dragged him to the door; the next morning, the three women brought him back by force to the old people's home; they harassed him as bees a drone half gone from the cold. The village would have been shocked if Dida had kept the no-good bum in her house—but who knows? Maybe Father Cicca would say it was sinful to chase him away. And because she is frugal and goes without, the cursed priest blames her for not loving herself enough. The weather is settling; but there are still flashes of lightning low on the horizon, at the end of streets, and this time on the Ponte Porzio side. Dida puts her hand on the little leather pouch hidden by her dress; it hangs from her neck like the gland of a goat—she thinks about Marinunzi and his knife. Maybe, at this very moment, lightning has struck the greenhouse, or a prowler is sneaking in to set it on fire, to make it look as if it did. On Judgment Day, God will burn up all the weeds.

Dida stuck her head out from under her shawl, cautiously, like a turtle, and peered into the darkness. Movies and cafés were now black houses. Puddles in holes in the pavement were only water from the sky. Two feet from Dida, a poor old devil who had seen better days dragged himself along the wall, ignoring the gutters, which dripped down on his cape from above. The street lamp at the entrance of the Conti Palace lit up his big pale eyes, his skimpy beard, the long hair under his shapeless hat. You might have taken him for the Good Lord fallen into poverty. In any case, he did not look dangerous; not one of those damned beggars who steal and set fires; on the contrary, on a night like this, it was a relief to see another living soul. The tramps Dida knew were bums not deserving of help; but this stranger seemed different. The beggar was going off after glancing at Dida like a man for whom faces have a sound like voices, and a meaning like words. Taking that glance as a call for help, Dida chooses this destitute man as the one to give alms to, the way a woman might more readily pick a chance lover, knowing her passion will be without entanglement.

Groping in her apron, she pulls out a ten-lira coin a customer in love had carelessly tossed her at the entrance to the movie theater, and presents it with great show to the needy man. 'Here, old man, this is for you.'

Startled, the man takes the coin, turns it over, then slips it in his pocket. Dida was afraid for a moment that her offering might be refused. He takes it: that's a good sign. Ten lire, she mumbles, you can't say *that's* nothing. And reassured, seeing that the thunder has stopped, with her conscience clear and squared with the invisible powers, she picks up her baskets and goes off to the courtyard of the Conti Palace for a nap.

Clement Roux removed his felt hat and mopped his forehead. He was soaked with rain and also with sweat. A limpid moon filled the new pure sky washed clean by the storm. An enchanted stillness reigned on the empty streets—here and there, gaps of light in shadowy passageways of celebrated sites offered glimpses of another world. The monuments seemed endowed with ageless youth or decrepitude; at the foot of a wall, a steel crane, with a block of stone between its teeth, looked like some antique catapult; pillar foundations and parts of columns scattered on the paving stones evoked a game that had ended, whose pawns in disarray hid an inescapable order; they seemed abandoned there by winners or losers who would never return.

Midnight struck; Clement's heart made its sick clock sound. Panting, he leaned against the railing of the Trajan Forum, which was still all torn up from recent excavations. Unsympathetic to these labors which devastated a near past for the profit of a more distant one, he leaned over and looked down into a space a few yards and a few centuries below ours, like one who, peering into an old grave reopened in the cemetery, fears to fall into it. His farsighted eyes looked in vain for the shiny pupils and light leaps of the many cats who used to prowl around the columns, fighting over the scraps thrown them by coachmen and British tourists; the animals evoked the image, on a smaller scale, of panthers playing with human bones in the arena. Disgusted, he remembered that they had been eliminated before the excavation had started. His discomfort increased, as if his angina were affected by their agonies. He had heard that only the common people were moved by the slaughter; a superstitious fear had made them predict the revenge of these wild little beasts; when the wife of the governor of Rome died tragically a few weeks later, they felt reassured by this expiation. Clement Roux thought as they did. Neither the time-immemorial prejudice that attributes a soul only to members of the human species nor the crass vanity that turns modern man into the upstart of nature had ever persuaded Clement that an animal is less worthy of God's solicitude than man. Wasn't the only thing that stuck from his Roman history lessons precisely the wild-beast attitudes of some of the emperors? These furry victims of municipal hygiene were as interesting to him as a stack of dead Caesars.

It's not as beautiful anymore, he thought, trying to divert his thoughts from the oppression growing inside him, which had reached the point where it gradually turned into pain. The ruins are too clean, too orderly . . . Too demolished, too reconstructed . . . In my day, these little streets zigzagged into the past and led you to the monument by surprise. They've replaced all that by magnificent thoroughfares for buses and, should the occasion arise, for tanks . . . Haussmann's Paris . . . the fairground of ruins, Permanent Exhibition of the Roman World . . . *Laudator temporis acti?* No, it's ugly. And in any case, too tiresome . . . This pain, really, is . . .

He breaks off his train of thought, stands still like an animal sensing danger. The vise is tightening . . . What is going to happen this time? . . . Is he going to fall down there? . . . He must be calm and try to deflect the crisis once more. The vials are in his left pocket.

The slight sound of an ampoule being broken. Amyl nitrate wafts through the air. Frowning, Clement carefully inhales the acidulous vapor that immediately relaxes his chest.

'Do you need anything?'

114

'Are you selling postcards?'

Forgetting his waning pain, Clement turned ill-temperedly toward the kindhearted passerby. Massimo's great beauty, being unexpected, startled him as if it had been a deformity.

'Never fear. I'm not selling anything tonight,' said the young man, with a contorted smile. 'Problems with your heart?'

Massimo held the old man up, then almost forced this big tired body to sit on a bench. The moonlight, the recent passing danger, this perfect profile leaning over him in the darkness—all this kept Clement in a world where cats are panthers and one is not surprised to be helped in French in the middle of Rome at night.

'Hell, I'm done for,' gasped the old man.

But this assertion came from someone who is already less afraid. The medication and the more powerful drug of a human presence had, once again, eased his anxiety: the crisis was coming to an end as suddenly as it had started, leaving in its wake a fatigue that was almost euphoric and a vague fear of the next time. The young man leaned against the low wall of the excavation. Out of habit, Clement noted the exhausted face of his companion, the shaking fingers which tried to make the cigarette lighter work. He looks as if he just pulled off a bad job, he thought. Never mind, it's good he's here. The young man smoked avidly. Clement Roux held out his hand.

'No . . . It's not good for you.'

'That's true,' he answered with humility. 'But I feel better . . . Unfortunately, with every false alarm . . . Ready for the worst . . . You don't understand that, do you? . . . How old are you?'

'I'm twenty-two.'

'That's what I thought. Me, I'm seventy.'

Twenty-two . . . no, twenty-two hundred, Massimo thought. She died a hundred years ago, Carlo, five hundred. Dead. Gone. This woman whose breathing I heard next to me on the pillow, this hand in my hand . . . And

115

him with his gasping breath and his gray suit we took to a Viennese tailor to be mended, his passion for German music ... A sum whisked off that total. *Inconceivable.* No explanation could ... This old man recovering from his heart pain doesn't know that he's solid ground for me, someone alive ...

'It's been thirty years since I had seen Rome ... Changed for the worst, ugly, like everything else ... Oh, I guess a young fellow like you finds in this some sort of beauty you'll miss too in thirty years. Nothing of the kind for me ... I hate noise ... I despise crowds ... And tonight I couldn't stand it in their Caesar Palace reception rooms ... So I went alone on foot ...'

'Like everyone else,' said Massimo in a voice he could not keep from shaking, 'to hear a speech in Piazza Balbo.'

'Not on your life! Go watch people bray acclamations to a howling man? You don't know me, my friend. No, but dark streets. Deserted ... Precisely because the crowd is poured out one side, like a pail being emptied. And then the angry rain on the buildings ... And me under an arch of the Coliseum, smoking, left in peace. Then, a little lost in these changed streets ... But the funniest thing is that not everything disappears at the same speed. I found certain corners, balconies, doors, things I didn't remember because they didn't seem worth it, but I do remember them when I see them, I recognize them ... And then putting my feet down on the pavement a little more carefully than before, you see, and feeling its unevenness more, its wear and tear. Am I boring you?'

'You're not boring me, Mr. Roux. I am thinking about a small painting of yours, an early one, which shows a corner of Rome, a landscape of very human ruins ... Even considering everything you've done since then, it's still very beautiful. Or was already very beautiful.' The poor great man, he thought, a little admiration will do him good.

'You know who I am?'

'It's very simple: the other day I saw your self-portrait

116

at the Triennial Exhibition of Modern Art.'

. . . And I'm getting used to it, he thought. I'm already accustomed to their death enough to be able to talk about painting. And besides I'm flattering him. I only recognized him because of the newspaper pictures.

'Well then, all joking aside, you know a poor bastard . . .' A kind of almost Belgian humming gave each sentence the aspect of a sad refrain. 'You're French? No, Russian. I know the accent. Me, I'm from Hazebrouck. Because you've got to be from somewhere. The portrait isn't bad: you have taste. Portraits, no one does them anymore, because people don't give a damn. Furthermore, it's too difficult. You have to take a face, pull it apart, put it back together, add up a series of spontaneous moments . . . Not your face: you're too handsome. It's not worth it. But a mug like mine . . . Your landscape of very human ruins, as you call it. You're very lucky to be twenty-two years old.'

Lucky, Massimo screamed silently, lucky . . . Talk about luck! To be the one who doesn't die, the one who watches, the one who never quite enters the game completely . . . The one who tries to save, or on the contrary . . . The angel of the last hours . . . And Marcella's look, I'll never forget it. Is it my fault if they love me? That hour stolen from time, at the end of everything . . . And I found nothing better to do than to begin by getting drunk on words . . . In order to encourage her, to hold her back . . . so be it. And mostly to hide that their world was not mine . . . The real betrayal was not to have yielded to that agent's blackmail in Vienna, during that business with the passports . . . Nor was it that obligatory visit last fall to a comic-opera character whose desk in Vedoni Palace had all those pigeonholes . . . No, you like the illicit . . . don't defend yourself, don't turn the thing into a gloomy joke . . . My name figures somewhere on their lists . . . Contaminated forever as by syphilis or leprosy . . . Live on, for forty years, with lingering symptoms of a forgiven infamy. Tomorrow I'll be summoned again by the comic-opera character; I'll be asked questions that I'll answer once again with the opposite of the truth. They're not so stupid . . . Only half stupid . . . They'll judge me as incompetent or as an accomplice. And, considering my status as a foreigner, they'll ask me to leave their lovely Italy, and to have my Nansen passport stamped elsewhere . . . Once again, my filthy luck . . . It will all boil down to a visit to my mother, who deals in antiques in Vienna.'

'What's the matter with you? You look like you're crying.'

No, I'm not crying, he thought savagely. I don't even have the right to cry for them.

'A woman was killed tonight. After the speech. It wasn't an accident. It was an attempted political act on her part.'

'Where?'

'Not far from here. On the little Piazza Santo Giovanni Martire.'

'Poor bitch,' Clement Roux murmured with respect.

Immediately Massimo thought: I was wrong to tell him. He's too old and too sick to worry about other people's misfortunes.

But the old man got up suddenly, anxious to be on his way. This remission won't last, he thought. Might as well take advantage of it to go home. Get away from here . . . And tomorrow leave Rome.

'Taxi?'

'Not right away . . . First I'd like . . . Besides, there aren't any.'

And expensive, he thought, this late at night. If this slightly shady but obliging youth would be willing to accompany me . . . I still have at least one vial on me. After all, it's probably nothing more than pseudoangina.

'Are you sure you can walk?'

'A little. It's rather good for me. It's not that far. Let's go by Piazza Santi Apostoli.'

They went by Piazza Santi Apostoli. He's proud that he still knows Rome so well, thought Massimo.

After a while, the old man stopped. 'About that woman. Were you there?'

'No,' said Massimo. 'No. No,' he screamed. '*No!*'

'And him? Is he unhurt?'

'Not a scratch,' answered Massimo bitterly. 'People say she missed by a hair.'

'What damned luck,' said Clement Roux with admiration. 'Oh, of course, sooner or later his luck will run out ... The risks of the job. In my youth, there was a popular refrain of Bruant about some sort of underwood thug: *He croaked like a Caesar* ... That's it: croak like a Caesar. I'm not saying that to belittle him; on the contrary ... Somebody's got to run things, since most people are too soft for the job. And you know, me and politics ... Besides, I'm not from here ... Only as long as he doesn't lead us to war.'

'Precisely,' said Massimo passionately. 'I'm not from here either.'

'I'll tell you what they make me think of, your politics,' said the old man. Then he stopped talking to cross an empty street very carefully. 'I have a friend who's director of the orchestra at La Scala. He told me that when they need crowd noises, the sounds of rebellion, people howling for or against, what have you, they get deep voices to sing from the wings one single beautiful, highly sonorous word: *rubarbara*. In rounds ... *barbararu* ... *bararubar* ... *rarubarba*. See what I mean? Well, politics, whether of the left or the right, it's *rubarbara* for me, my boy.'

Massimo was keeping step with the old man, who was dragging his feet. Raising his eyes, he noticed that the street they were walking on was Via dell'-Umilità. Humility Street, he repeated to himself.

'Mr. Clement Roux,' he said after a small hesitation, 'you were in the 1914 war. How did you get used to knowing that the comrades you lived with would perhaps in an hour ... almost without fail ... That woman, for example ... Well, she was a member of the same group ... The friend of a friend.' Would you dare say of a lover, he thought. It didn't make that much difference to me. And to him. A break with his background. A reaction against his leftist puritanism. A return to who knows what moment of his youth? And if it counted for more than that, it was in a realm words don't enter . . . More sincere by not saying it than by saying it. 'A friend,' he went on aloud. 'But I had introduced myself under false pretenses . . .' No, that is not quite the truth either, he thought, despairing of defining so awkwardly anything at all. From Kitzbühel on, I warned him; I even advised him never to go back to Italy. I couldn't do any more. But from that time on, the die was cast. 'A dead friend,' he went on aloud, more for himself than for his companion. 'And that woman, I followed her closely a while back. I learned about it by chance, at the entrance to a café, at a respectable distance from it all. Oh, I was free not to believe in the effectiveness of political assassination! All the same,' he said, turning away to hide his tears, 'she must have despised me as she died.'

What's he making up, thought the old man, alarmed. 'Well, my boy,' he said, 'I don't understand a word of your story. First of all, to begin with, where are you from? The gentleman conspires? No? So much the better . . . Do you have a family? I would say probably not. An address?'

'Until tomorrow morning.'

'I thought as much . . . And how do you make a living?'

'I deal in false passports,' said Massimo with a sneer.

'Ah . . . Well, then, my friend, you're out of luck with me . . . Even if I didn't have one in my pocket. Don't feel like going anywhere anymore. Unless you have one good enough to avoid any problems with God.'

'You mustn't say that,' said Massimo seriously.

Clement Roux had stopped walking and was leaning against a wall the top of which had a two-foot-high inscription counseling the citizens of Rome to live dangerously. This street, he thought, I'll probably never come here again . . . And Rome . . . I should look around me . . . All the more because it is, after all, really beautiful . . . The almost imperceptible curves of these buildings, rounding off space . . . Moreover, it will be better

120

than if I seem to keep stopping because I'm tired . . . Yet I feel very good . . . Incredibly good . . . In spite of it all, I'm walking as if I had the brake on. If something happened, this boy could always get help . . . Unless . . . The newspaper headlines tomorrow would read: Clement Roux found dead on the street of a heart attack, mugged by . . . No: not mean, unhappy, even slightly mythomaniac. Still, if a taxi comes by, it would be a good idea to flag it.

If a taxi comes by, it would be more prudent to have him take it, thought Massimo, who was tired. The last one was full.

'Speaking of the war of '14,' the old man said, walking on again. 'I was already too old . . . My brother's the one who got himself killed at Craonne. But they lied about it so much that even those who came back no longer know . . . And not only about the war, about life . . . Therefore, when the Italian reporters ask me about myself . . . My mother, she wanted me to be a priest. Picture her, the lady of the farm, in her plush hat to go to church in on winter Sundays . . . And then Paris, and work, and the usual struggles of the artist not making it, and the lousiness of it all. And then fame . . . For no reason, because the wind shifted. I never realized that there were that many art dealers in the world, and people who speculate in paintings. The Stock Exchange, the Outside Bettors . . . And those who used me to knock down the illustrious of the day before, so they can say that Renoir was no big deal, that Manet is warm beer. Then the time comes that you're so well known that nobody cares anymore: Clement Roux, classified. And in ten years people will stick the paintings in their damned attics, because they'll be out of fashion; and in fifty years they'll hang in museums, even those that are forgeries, and in two hundred years people will say that Clement Roux never existed, that it was really someone else, or that there were several Roux. And in a thousand years there will be nothing left but a couple of inches of a canvas so badly damaged that you won't be able to tell what it is anymore, the great Clement Roux, the unique work, painted, glazed over, scoured, remounted, and moreover, maybe forged . . . My fame . . . Where was I? My memories. My wife, an excellent woman, the best of wives . . . Good housekeeper, not even jealous . . . and pretty to begin with; the whitest body imaginable; like milk. Of course, you know her, I painted her. Two years of love; a child with a little white collar in the paintings of 1905, who now sells cars; another child who died . . . And the lady growing old, losing weight, becoming difficult (always the proper lady, you know), you no longer feel like making love to her, no more than you would to a church-club matron . . . Yes, I also painted her in that mode, in a gray dress. And then she died . . . What a change . . . You get used to it . . . You get used to not getting used to it. And your fellow countrywoman, Sabine Bagration, who takes it into her head to love me, and moves me into her villa on the Riviera, and our quarrels, and she threatens me with a gun. A woman with a sallow complexion, slim, not beautiful, but interesting. A woman who loves unhappiness, like you. And she had plenty of it; in her country, she got herself thrown down a mine shaft . . . What else? . . . All in all, I didn't live that much . . . Painting really takes a lot of discipline. You have to get up early . . . Go to bed early . . . I don't have any memories.'

A second taxi went by which neither one of them flagged down. The moon had taken on that evil aspect it assumes in the late hours, when one isn't used to being outdoors and everything looks different in the sky. Their footsteps rang out in the empty street. And this is what the old dotard covered with fame got out of life, thought Massimo . . . of course, there's always his masterpieces . . . And you, where will you be at his age? Even in ten years? A hotel employee? A correspondent for an evening newspaper? An aging Narcissus who looks into shop windows to see if adventure will come his way? . . . Or perhaps a fanatic passing out pamphlets about the coming of the Lord? . . . Don't worry . . . Wait . . .

Accept even this sensual incompatibility: she was closer to you than any woman will ever be, but you couldn't stand the oily, spicy smell of her hair . . . Accept not having quite believed in what they did . . . Accept the fact that they are dead: you too will die someday. Accept (since you must) being tainted with infamy . . . Wait . . . Start from what you are . . . Right now you are walking back to his hotel a poor great man in an artsy costume of the years 1900 . . . Out of faithfulness to his youth? . . . So conventional, these French people . . .

'Mr. Roux,' he said, free to renew his attempt since he no longer hoped to be listened to. 'This dead friend . . . Carlo Stevo . . .'

'Yes, I know who Carlo Stevo is,' the painter said absentmindedly.

'I know this can't really interest you,' he went on in a shaky voice, 'but still, it's a little like your memories. No one understands . . . And oblivion comes so quickly. Oh, they talk about Carlo Stevo; they'll talk about him even more tomorrow when they find out he's dead. But without knowing . . . A great writer, a genius misled by politics, will say those who are not insulting him . . . All this noise about a wretched, extorted letter, but no one, not even me, who can envisage brutalities, physical suffering, weariness, doubts at the very moment of death . . . No, no one. His letter was so cautious, it didn't reveal anything essential; it discredited the government just when it seemed to ask for mercy . . . subtle . . . But they don't understand that a dying man is willing to look as if he is yielding, as if he is giving up what he thought he believed in; that he might be willing to die alone, even without convictions, all alone . . . Carlo Stevo, and his courage to go all the way on everything, to the limits of his strength, beyond that strength . . . To succumb with shame, to be ridiculous . . . To speak German badly, for example . . . His capacity to understand, his incapacity to despise . . . His wonderful feeling for Beethoven: those evenings in the room in Spiegelgasse when we played all the records of the last quartets . . . His cheer-

fulness of a sad man . . . And if I have been the only one
to follow, to share, to give someone this brief happiness
those who say they love him never gave? . . . And his
books, so often mentioned, no longer read . . . In the long
run, I'm the only one left as witness . . . Had he lived, I
would have learned something perhaps . . . *Tzarstvo
tebe nebesnoe,*' he ended, not realizing he was reciting
the prayer for the dead in ecclesiastic Old Slavonic.

'Well, well,' said Clement Roux. 'Well, well . . .'

Turning the corner of a narrow street, they came suddenly into a small piazza that was no more than the
basin of a fountain. Marble gods presided over this
trickling; whirlpools, eddies, quiet puddles had formed
in the hollows of sculptured stone rocks that time,
humidity, and erosion had transformed into real rocks.
A baroque fancy, a mythological opera prop had gradually become a great natural monument that offered, at
the heart of the city, rock and water both older and
younger than Rome.

'My God, how beautiful,' said Clement Roux. 'Help me
to go down the step . . . It's very slippery. I'd like to sit for
a while on the rim.'

Massimo remained standing. Water that washes, he
thought, water that assumes and erases all forms . . .
water that was perhaps denied someone suffering from
fever, there, on Lipari Island . . . An almost forgotten
memory came back to him, overwhelmingly real, super-
imposing itself on this piazza, on this fountain, on this old
man sitting on the step. The water of the river, the
immense liquid mass he sailed down on with his mother
and their companions during the dangerous voyage
undertaken to escape from their native country. He sees
again the islands submerged by spring flooding, hears
the cuckoos calling out to each other from opposite
banks; the feeling of a brand-new, limitless adventure,
his delight, contrasting with the fear and discomfort of
the adults. At night they slept in abandoned farms, being
careful to lie flat on the ground, on straw. Sometimes a
cavalry squad would come by; the men sang, or absent-

mindedly distracted themselves by shooting at windows reflecting the moonlight. Stray bullets, he thought. What makes me think of those stray bullets?

'You see,' said the old man, 'I wouldn't want you to think ... There are some worthwhile things ... Things that you should want to ... This fountain, for example. I wanted to see it again before leaving, but on these tiny streets you're never sure to find anything again ... Things so beautiful that you're surprised they are there. Fragments, bits ... Paris, gray all over. Rome, golden ... That column over there, where we were, did you notice, like a moon dial? And the Coliseum, that is really something, isn't it, the Coliseum, a well-baked pâté with a thick stone crust, stuffed with gladiators inside ... And the water spouts like living obelisks ... And there, everywhere, anything, a coffeepot or a cathedral ... And wonderful faces, like yours ... And bodies ...'

Lowering his head, he scooped up some water in his hand and watched it slip through his thick fingers. He went on: 'Women's bodies ... Not models, nude for so much per hour ... Nor the insipid nakedness of hookers, nor the nakedness of burlesque that is covered with so much makeup you can no longer see the skin ... And the women of my day, who had the marks of their corset stays all over their torsos, and the women of today, with their girdles, as they call them, and a little roll of fat around the waist, like gooseflesh. And virtually not a perfect foot among them, firm and pure ... But from time to time a bit of skin glimpsed under a piece of clothing like a sweet secret in this hard world ... The body behind the material ... The soul behind the body ... The body's soul ... Once, a long time ago, on a deserted beach in Sicily, a little naked girl ... Twelve or thirteen ... In the faint daylight of early morning ... She took off her camisole when she saw me, because she wanted to show herself, I guess. Innocent and yet not innocent ... Can you picture it, a little Venus emerging from the waves ... Her legs a little paler than the rest of her, because you saw them underwater ... Oh, don't think

125

that I . . . too young, and too beautiful . . . Even though I could have, after all . . . And I didn't paint her either, because nudes painted from memory . . . But I put her, here and there, everywhere, in a certain way of showing light playing on a body. These are things that help when your time to die has come.'

His hands clumsily lifted the collar of his cloak, as if he were suddenly cold. 'I think . . . I think I'm catching a cold,' he stammered.

'You have to go home, Mr. Clement Roux. It's after one o'clock.'

'Yes,' he said. 'I understand . . . Closing time, gentlemen . . . I'm coming, but not right away . . . Don't be impatient. First I must finish Baroness Bernheim's portrait . . . I'm going back to France. Dr. Sarte . . .'

Massimo gave a start. Clement noticed but paid no attention. Lost in his thoughts, he went on. '. . . says that this country is no good for me in this season . . . The first hot spells . . . I hope the valet secured my trunk firmly . . . The ten-fifteen train. But first . . .'

And convulsively squeezing Massimo's fingers, he went on in a more confidential tone: 'It's hard to leave just when you're beginning to understand, when you've learned . . . And you go on painting, you add forms to this world full of forms . . . In spite of fatigue. And I used to be in strapping health, you know, like a farm boy . . . And even today, on the days I feel well, I feel eternal . . . Only, when things go wrong, there is now someone in me who says yes. Says yes to death . . .'

His drivel became like drunkenness. He took the ten-lira coin out of his pocket, turned it over in the palm of his hand. 'During the rain shower, as I told you,' he said, 'I took cover under an arch. Soaked, nevertheless . . . A kind old woman must have mistaken me for a beggar. She gave me this . . . Isn't it funny? . . . Oh, don't misunderstand me: she wasn't drunk . . . Maybe it was restitution.'

He's the one who's drunk, thought Massimo with disgust. Drunk with fatigue. This grotesque, this pitiful funeral vigil.

126

'And those travelers leaving, if they throw a coin in the water,' the old painter went on in his inexhaustible, senile verbiage, 'it is said they'll come back . . . Yes. But as far as I'm concerned, considering what I would be doing in Rome, I'm not tempted to come back. Rather see something else, something really new, with fresh eyes, eyes washed clean, pure eyes . . . But what else is there? Who's really seen the Eternal City? Life, my friend, maybe life starts only after the Resurrection.'

'Come on, Mr. Clement Roux, are you coming?'

'Yes,' said the old man.

He threw the coin awkwardly; it landed two feet from him, in the nook of a rock.

'It would have been better to have given it to me,' Massimo couldn't help saying.

'You want my money?'

'I want to take you home,' the young man said firmly. Let's get it over with, he thought with despair. But I can't leave him stranded like this, with his feet on the wet ground.

This time, gripping Massimo's arm, Clement got up. Massimo held him upright. Suddenly, raising frightened eyes to look at him, the old man stammered: 'I don't feel well . . . Wait a minute.'

'I'll go get you a taxi,' said Massimo, alarmed, sitting the sick man again on the rim of the fountain. 'Piazza Colonna is just around the corner . . .'

'Don't leave me alone,' protested the old man.

But he was already alone. He was forced to stay seated, concentrating on a pain that seemed to branch out, spread, fill a third of his left arm. Controlling his terror, Clement looked at the empty piazza all around him. Except for a worker doing emergency repairs on a water leak on the street, there was no one there. The little hotel Clement knew across from the fountain is closed at this hour, its door and windows dark. Moreover, he knows that he is incapable of taking those few steps, as he would be to cross Rome itself. He tries in vain to belch to get some relief. The water and rock, so wonderful a little while ago, are now only insensible substances that can't help him. The music of the waterfall is only a noise that would cover up his calls for help were he capable of screaming.

Then the stranglehold loosens up a bit. The news of a reprieve is, once again, mysteriously conveyed from the very depths of his body. Perhaps it won't be tonight after all, he thinks. And, in resignation, head down, he waits for the pain to cease altogether, or to return and carry him off.

He didn't wait long. After a minute, a car approached almost soundlessly; it stopped at the edge of the fountain. Massimo was sitting next to the driver. He jumped down, helped the old man to get up, and almost carried him into the car. 'To Caesar Palace, right?'

Clement Roux nodded.

'To Caesar Palace,' Massimo said to the driver.

Avoiding the Water Works repairs, the car moved in reverse for a moment before driving off into Via Stamperia. For a brief second, the headlight hit the young man, who was standing at the curb, right in the face; it showed features that suddenly seemed less pure; it revealed the dirt on the white shirt, the wrinkles on the crumpled jacket. Seized suddenly by a worry that this time had nothing mysterious about it, Clement felt for his wallet: it was there. He immediately became anxious again, as if there were something here that couldn't be explained. He muttered: 'I should have asked him for his name.'

He knocked on the glass pane to tell the driver to turn around. The man didn't hear him. Massimo's pale face had already disappeared into the night. Exhausted, Clement Roux sat back in his corner and closed his eyes, already on his way out of Rome. He was happy to have been put in the driver's care by the stranger; the driver would soon turn him over to the hotel doorman; once again having assumed the reassuring routine of day-to-day reality, Clement Roux felt safe.

It was dark on the plains, in the hills, dark in the city, dark on the islands, and dark on the sea. Half the world was inundated with darkness. It was dark on the second-class deck of the boat from Palermo where Paolo Farina, letting his leather briefcase slip off his lap, mingled his snoring with the murmurs of the Sea of Sicily. Anesthetized by the dark, Rome seemed to be situated on the banks of the river Lethe. Caesar slept, forgetting he was Caesar. He woke up, slipped inside his person and his fame, looked at the time, and rejoiced to have shown, during the incident of the day before, the composure befitting a statesman. Ardeati, born Ardeati, he thinks, pondering the name he had them spell out for him a few hours ago, old Giacomo's daughter . . . And he sees again, from a great distance, the kitchen of the Cesena apartment, hears again a discussion about the comparative merits of Marx and Engels, and smells the coffee Mother Ardeati served in the days when for him coffee was a rare treat. I amalgamated into my program what was best in these people, he tells himself. Those windbags would never have been able to govern the nation. And he turns over on his pillow, at peace with himself, certain of the approval of law-and-order people.

Giulio Lovisi is not asleep; he is going over his accounts, leaning on a bolster on his bed, and annoyed by Giuseppa and Vanna's whispers. The two women are talking feverishly, never-endingly, on the other side of the wall, about the chances of Carlo's immediate return—a sobered-up Carlo, thinking like everyone else, won back to good principles and reconciled with the great man. Mother and daughter talk in the dark, afraid of waking up the child, who, however, is not asleep. The little invalid, sensing the excitement of the adults, is irritated at being excluded, asks for a glass of lemonade to call attention to herself. Alessandro is not asleep either. Detained at the all-night political headquarters, pale, drained with fatigue, but very much in control of himself, he explains to a highly placed official what he knows of his wife's whereabouts these last few months; that is to say, almost nothing. An obliging night watchman brings the gentlemen glasses of water.

Don Ruggero was asleep in his asylum, and his dreams were no different from those sane people dream. Lina Chiari was in bed with her cancer; she dreamed of Massimo, who was not dreaming of her. The dead were also asleep, but no one knew what they were dreaming of. In a room at the Caesar Palace, Clement Roux is resting from his long stroll; he is wallowing in a still-life of yawning suitcases, shoes strewn anywhere, flannel sweaters thrown over the arms of chairs. He is feeling better; he is sleeping gluttonously; his old slack body is a mass of gray flesh and gray hair. In the next room, an electric night lamp that looks like a big firefly that might have come in through the half-open window sheds soft light on a sleeping woman; a luxurious darkness suffuses the room where Angiola dozes in the sheets of Angiola Fides. Her peaceful face, without makeup, covered here and there by moving strands of hair, has the innocent beauty of her breasts and bare arms. Alessandro's roses lie in the bathroom basin, at the edge of a puddle of water. The impecunious Miss Jones missed her train because she did not want to leave the Cinema Mondo before the end of the movie; she sleeps fitfully in the squalid room she rented right next to the railway station. Dida sleeps like a hen between her two baskets in the courtyard of the Conti Palace; her Tullia and her Maria, back to back under their threadbare but clean blanket, are enjoying what is left to them of the night before they must go down to the field and the greenhouse; Ilario wonders, but not too anxiously, what could have happened to the old woman.

Toward two in the morning, Massimo ate a sandwich and had bitter black coffee in a snack bar about to close, near the train station. Home now in his furnished room in Via San Niccolò da Tolentino, he sleeps, half dressed, lying across the bed like a breathing, warm statue of a young god. Suddenly the boy wakes up, hesitates for a moment at the edge of consciousness, then covers his face with his elbow as if struck by a memory. He gets up, kicks under the bed the suitcase he had dragged into the middle of the room; he doesn't want to give the impression that he is running away. But he gets ready to leave, mentally. Seeing the open closet, he can't help thinking it's a good thing he had a suit made by Duetti before leaving Rome. Ashamed of that thought as if it were obscene, he walks up to the pseudo-chimney shelf where his books lie. A Shestov, a Berdyaev, a German translation of a volume of Kierkegaard, Apollinaire's *Alcools*, *Das Studenbuch* by Rilke, and two works by Carlo Stevo. I can't take any of these, he thinks. Then, changing his mind, he weighs in his hands the two books by his friend, chooses the slimmer one, slips it among the objects to be taken along, and, overcome with weariness, falls asleep again sitting by the table, head in his hands.

In the museums of Rome, darkness fills the rooms that house the masterpieces: *The Sleeping Fury, The Hermaphrodite, The Anadyomene Venus, The Dying Gladiator*, marble blocks obeying the great general laws that rule the equilibrium, the weight, the density, the dilation, and the contraction of stones; they will never know that artisans, dead for thousands of years, fashioned their surface to the image of creatures of another realm. The ruins of ancient monuments are an integral part of the night, privileged fragments of the past, safe behind their gate with the empty chair of the guard next

131

to the entrance turnstile. At the Triennial Exhibition of Modern Art, the paintings are now only rectangular framed pieces of canvas caked with a layer of colors that right now is black. On the slopes of the Capitol, in her lair behind bars, the wolf howls at the night; protected from humans but made uneasy by their proximity, she doesn't know that she is a symbol, and shudders at the vibration of the truck that now and then drives by the foot of the hill. It's that time of night when, in stables contiguous to slaughterhouses, animals who tomorrow will wind up on dinner plates and in the sewers lean their soft and sleepy muzzles on the necks of their fettered companions. It's that time of night when the sick who can't sleep lie in hospitals, impatiently waiting for the night nurse's next round. It's that time of night when the girls in the brothel sitting room tell themselves that soon they'll be able to go to sleep. In newspaper printshops, the presses are turning, grinding out for the morning readers a manipulated version of yesterday's events; true or false, news crackles in telephone receivers; gleaming rails traced patterns of departures in the dark.

Along the streets, from the top to the bottom of each dark house, sleepers are stacked like the dead along the sides of catacombs; spouses sleep bearing in their damp and warm bodies the living beings of the future, the rebels, the resigned, the violent, the swindlers, the saints, the idiots, the martyrs. A vegetal darkness unfolds and shudders in the pine trees of the Pincio and the Villa Borghese; they are all that is left of formerly immense patrician gardens, ravaged by devastating speculations that fell on cities. The song of the fountains rises purer and keener in the silence of the night; and at Piazza di Trevi, where a black flood overran the foot of the stone Neptune, Oreste Marinunzi, the laborer from the Water Works, having repaired the leak, climbed over the railing of the basin, stuck his two hands into the crag of a rock, and raking at random, took out some coins thrown in the water by fools.

*   *   *

He was somewhat disappointed; his catch was meager; the biggest coin was only ten lire; one would think there were fewer tourists now, or that they had become poorer. For a moment, he thought of calling some of the gang back to buy them a round of drinks, but his luck did not warrant this bountifulness; they were already a distance away, and besides, it wasn't a good idea to let too many people in on the fountain business. With what he had, he could buy himself, at most, a tie for the christening, or one or two bottles of Asti for the family to drink the health of the mother of the newborn. That is, if everything went well: Oreste Marinunzi mentally proffered something like a prayer to the divinities of pregnancy. To tell the truth, neither Attilia nor he needed this fourth one, but when children come, what can you do? Around eight o'clock, Oreste had left their Trastevere two-room apartment, now turned inside out—basins of water, broth, coffee being heated up by the neighbors, votive candles burning before the Madonna, lots of excited, chattering women, and Attilia streaming with sweat, very pale, her hair unraveled. It was not an occasion when a man enjoys going home.

Ignoring his soaked trousers, he walked with the assured gait of a regular customer to a little bar next to the train station where friends of the owner could drink all night long without worrying about closing time. It's not that he was a bad husband; on the contrary: it was better to let the women manage on their own. As soon as he had gone through the door and the bead curtain that served as a door in the summer, Oreste noticed with chagrin that it wasn't the owner, a good fellow, dozing behind the counter, but his nephew, who always wound up picking a quarrel with you. The room was virtually empty, except for a handful of railroad workers whom he didn't know, and two Germans in shorts, knapsacks between their legs. Oreste sat down with his back to them because he did not like to be looked at, from top to bottom, by foreigners; he ordered a bottle of Genzano wine and got ready to drink it as a connoisseur, with a knowledgeable air.

The wine was not of the best quality, but it was drinkable nevertheless. The first bottle gave him back his self-confidence: Attilia would have an easy time of it, because there was a full moon. He himself did not believe in those feminine superstitions, but at times like this, it was reassuring to think of them. According to the fortune-teller, the fourth would be a boy like the other three; they were easier to bring up than girls; boys serve their country, and they can end up being a big sports celebrity in the newspapers someday. He looked around him: the wall was decorated with the dictator's photograph pinned to the wall with three thumbtacks, and a poster showing a pretty girl from Amalfi gathering oranges in her apron. Oreste raised his glass to the health of the Chief of State: in his youth, he had been a regular subscriber to the Socialist Party: he could have put that money to better use by drinking it away. Now in his position as head of the household, he adhered to the party of law and order: he knew how to fittingly honor a truly great man, a man who spoke loud and clear, who shows foreigners what's what, and who would make the country really count in the next war. Children, you needed children to build a great nation.

The second bottle was better than the first. The distance between him and the room where Attilia was screaming in the hands of her neighbors suddenly doubled. A handsome woman, Attilia, as handsome in her way as the girl with the oranges, but there isn't exactly a shortage of handsome women. And indeed, a pretty blonde had just come in with a suitcase; she sat down against the wall, on the chair next to the door, like a woman slightly afraid of being there alone. The bead curtain caught in her hair; she gave a startled cry, then freed herself. Oreste rose gallantly to come to her aid. Frightened, Miss Jones turned her eyes away from this drunken man. Her economical local train did not leave until the early hours of the morning. She had gotten up too early, scared by noises coming from the next room; the waiting room of the train station would have been a

134

refuge, but at this unsafe hour she was afraid to cross the street again carrying her suitcase.

Miss Jones was leaving this country all the poets and novelists of England had led her to, without regrets. In Sicily, she had struggled with lazy servants, strange food, waterless faucets, and the horror of little birds slaughtered by the rifles of skillful hunters under the flowering almond trees of Gemara. Rome had been spoiled for her by the anxious wait for a check, by the insulting scene a woman who was no lady made in a Corso shop, and by the amorous glances of men whose advances seemed to this frail little nymph both an affront and a danger. She hoped Gladys, her old friend, would not object to sharing the sleeping couch of her London apartment with her again. She was homesick for her morning toast, her evening tea, for the cheap seats at fashionable shows, for Gladys's sentimental accounts of her love life, her reassuring affection, bordering on friendship and sweet love. And looking at her watch every five minutes, Miss Jones dreamed of gray skies in the way that, a few months from now, she would bitterly regret blue ones.

Oreste sat down again, which seemed the safer thing to do. The pretty Englishwoman didn't seem quite as young as he had thought. 'They're not really women,' he grumbled. Attilia, by comparison, rose in value again: it wasn't her fault that her old mother was too stingy and would not help with the payments for the wardrobe or let them get the dishes back from the pawnshop. He thought he had married into a family that had money, but that sneaky Ilario would inherit everything; Dida would probably not leave Attilia enough even to buy mourning clothes with. A gentle sadness emanated from the bottom of the second bottle. People did not recognize his true worth; because one day, when he had too much to drink, he happened to mention that it would be nice to cut his mother-in-law's throat, they treated him now as

135

an assassin, him, Oreste Marinunzi, who wouldn't hurt a fly. And that sneaky Ilario took advantage of the situation to drive him off without so much as an offer of a glass when he came to Ponte Porzio. Voluptuously, he pictured strangling the old woman; he invented precise details, savored the pleasure of grabbing the little leather pouch right under her nose, the pouch that held the fortune that should have been his and Attilia's children's. But such acts of justice always lead to prison; judges never understand how mistreated one has been by the people one kills. He sighed, putting the scene back in the drawer for dreams, next to the scene in which he tells the Director of the Water Works what he thinks of him (the man refused to give him a raise), and next to the scene where he talks back to Attilia, who accuses him of being a drunk, and the scene where he chews out the neighborhood butcher for hugging Attilia too tightly. And to console this Oreste to whom nobody showed the proper respect, he ordered some rum with his third bottle.

Thereupon, a modification, like a shifting of gears, occurred in the rhythm of his drunkenness. It was no longer a question of drinking to drink but to arrive at a supreme moment, as with a woman, to reach a sublime state where Oreste Marinunzi no longer counted. A splendor only he could see covered him like a purple cloak; wild grapes were tangled in his hair. The first gulp turned him into the legitimate heir of Old Mother Dida and the owner of Ponte Porzio; he and Attilia and the four kids would settle in the country; Tullia, Maria, and that sneaky Ilario had suddenly vanished, eliminated from the universe by an act of divine will; precariously balanced on three feet of his chair, Oreste Marinunzi got drunk in peace under a bower. All the water pipes of Rome could sprout leaks, he would not be bothered. Happy as a rich man, he became kind. Ilario and his shitface sisters were allowed to occupy the shanty at the bottom of the garden. He wished the railroad workers, the Germans, and the Englishwoman well (she wasn't so bad, after all); the owner's nephew, who at this very moment was deciding to kick him out, suddenly seemed a friend, a real one, on whom you could rely as much as, even more than, on a brother. The third gulp made him powerful: he felt obliged to rise and deliver a great speech like the one of the day before, and Oreste Marinunzi, having doubled salaries, lowered the cost of living, won a war, and earned his place in the sun forever, sat down again, happy as a king, or rather, a dictator.

With the fourth gulp, ideas of the kind he usually didn't have came to him. He looked at the calendar praising the virtues of a certain brand of bitters, and wondered what was the meaning of day, of month, of year; he thought that the first flies of the season, which were hanging from the sticky paper trap, feebly trying to wrench themselves free, were very funny; happy to remember his school lessons, he told himself that, all in all, it was like that, upside down, that men walked on this big turning ball. Everything was, in fact, turning now: a majestic waltz carried off the walls, the calendar with the bitters ad, the portrait of the Chief of State, and his own hand that was trying without success to steady the bottle. One more gulp and his eyes closed as if darkness were preferable to the spectacle of a tavern. The back of his chair, leaning against the wall, slipped; he landed on the ground without realizing that he had fallen, and lay there, happy as a dead man.

THE END

Afterword

A first, somewhat shorter version of *Denier du rêve (A Coin in Nine Hands)* appeared in 1934. The present novel is much more than a simple reprint, or even a second, corrected edition enlarged with previously unpublished passages. Some chapters have been almost entirely rewritten and sometimes considerably developed; in certain sections the corrections, the cuts, the transpositions, have left almost no line unchanged; in other sections, however, large segments of the 1934 version appear intact. The novel, such as it is today, is half original text and half reconstruction from the years 1958-59, but in that reconstruction the old and the new overlap to such an extent that it is almost impossible, even for the author, to tell where one begins and the other ends.

Not only have the characters, the names, the personalities, the relationships, and the settings remained the same, but the main and secondary themes of the book, its structure, the starting point of the episodes, and most often their outcome, have also not changed. The novel still has as its center the half-realistic, half-symbolic story of an attempted anti-Fascist assassination in Rome in the year XI of the dictatorship. As before, a certain number of tragicomic characters, sometimes linked to the main drama, sometimes totally divorced from it, but almost all more or less consciously affected by the conflicts and slogans of their times, are grouped around three or four heroes of the central episode. What also belongs to the first version of *Denier du rêve* is the choice of people, who, at first glance, seem to be escapees from a *commedia* or rather a modern *tragedia dell'arte*; these people were selected to underline their most particular, most irreducibly singular qualities, or to suggest a personal *quid divinum* even more essential in them than their own nature. The tendency toward myth or allegory was somewhat similar in the two versions; it attempted to meld into one picture the Rome of the year XI of the Fascist era and the city where the eternal human story is set and unraveled. Finally, the deliberate stereotype structural element—the coin passing from hand to hand, to link episodes by the reappearance of the same characters, the same themes, or the introduction of complementary themes—was part of the first version of the book. In that version the ten-lira coin, the coin of the dream (the *denier du rêve*), became, as in this book, the symbol of contact between human beings each lost in his own passions and in his intrinsic solitude. In partially rewriting *Denier du rêve*, I say almost exactly the same thing, though sometimes in different terms.

But, if that is the case, why undertake such a major reconstruction? The answer is very simple. As I reread the novel, certain passages seemed to me too deliberately elliptic, too vague, too ornate, too tense or too slack, and sometimes just badly done. The modifications that make of the 1959 version a different book from the 1934 one are all introduced in order to create a more complete, hence more particularized presentation of certain episodes, to allow a more penetrating psychological development, to simplify and clarify, and if possible, to enrich and add depth to the text. In some places, I tried to enlarge the role of realism; elsewhere, that of poetry—in the long run, these are, or should be, the same thing. The switch from prose virtually to poetry, the abrupt transitions from drama to comedy to satire have been increased. I had already used the stylistic devices of direct and indirect narration, dramatic dialogue, and sometimes even lyrical passages resembling arias; I added now, on rare occasions, the device of interior monologue—not, as almost always in contemporary novels, to show a mind-mirror passively reflecting the flood of images and impressions flowing past, but reduced here to the basic elements of personage, or almost to the simple alternation of yes and no . . .

I could multiply these examples, which are more likely to interest writers of novels than readers, but I won't. Let me at least dispute the validity of the prevalent opinion that taking an older work and retouching or partly rewriting it is a useless or even injurious enterprise because it destroys the original impulse and passion. On the contrary, for me it was both a privilege and an experience to see this substance, fixed on the page for such a long time, become once again pliable, to relive this adventure I had made up in circumstances I no longer even remembered, and finally to find myself again before these romanesque events as before situations I had already lived through once. Now, however, I could explore them better, interpret them or explain them more fully, even though it was not in my power to change them. The opportunity of expressing ideas and emotions that were still mine, with improved craftsmanship and through the insights gleaned from a longer human experience, seemed to me too precious not to be accepted with joy and humility.

All in all, it is the political climate of the story that has changed least in the book, since the events of this novel, which occur in Rome, are quite precisely dated the eleventh year of the Fascist era. These few imaginary events, such as Carlo's deportation and death, Marcella's attempted assassination of Mussolini, are placed, therefore, in 1933; that is, during times when arbitrary laws against enemies of the regime had been multiplying for several years, times when a few such political assassinations had been attempted. Furthermore, all this occurs before the expedition into Ethiopia, before the regime's participation in the Spanish Civil War, before the alliance with and quick subjugation to

Hitler, before the promulgation of racial laws, and, of course, before the years of confusion, disaster, but also heroic partisan resistance during World War II. It was important, then, not to confuse the image of 1933 with the darker one of the years that saw the conclusion of what had been germinating in 1922–33. Marcella's gesture had to remain a quasi-individual, tragically isolated protest; her ideology had to show the influence of those anarchistic doctrines that once so deeply marked Italian dissidence; Carlo Stevo had to keep his political idealism so limited and futile in appearance; and the regime itself had to keep its alleged positive and triumphant aspect, since it deceived, for such a long time, not so much the Italian people as the outside world. One of the reasons that *Denier du rêve* seemed worthy to be published again is that, in its day, it was one of the first French novels (maybe the very first) to confront the hollow reality behind the bloated façade of Fascism, this at a time when so many writers visiting the country were happy still to be enchanted by the traditional Italian picturesqueness, or to applaud the trains running on time (at least in theory), without wondering what terminals the trains were running toward.

Like all the themes in the book, the political one is reinforced and developed in the present version. Carlo Stevo's story takes up more pages, but all the circumstances had appeared briefly or were implicit in the earlier version. The repercussions of the political drama on secondary characters are more deeply etched. Unlike in the first book, Marcella's attempted coup and her death are commented upon, not only by Dida, the old flower vender, and by Clement Roux, the foreign traveler, but also by the only two new minor characters introduced into the book—the owner of the café and the dictator himself. Here, however, Mussolini remains what he was in the earlier book, a huge political shadow cast over Italy; politics now excite the drunken Marinunzi almost as much as the bottle. Finally, Alessandro and Massimo, each in his own way, became stronger witnesses to the events.

Perhaps no one will be surprised that political evil plays a bigger part in this version than it did in the older one, or that the *Denier du rêve* of 1959 is more bitter or more ironic than the one of 1934. Rereading the new parts of the book as though someone else had written them, however, I'm especially cognizant of the fact that the text is now both a little more scathing and a little less dark, that certain judgments about human nature are perhaps less cutting and yet less vague, and that dream and reality, the two principal elements in the book, are no longer separate, or almost irreconcilable, but now seem merged to form a unity that is, after all, life. No correction is ever purely formal. The feeling that the human story is even more tragic, if that's possible, than we suspected a quarter of a century ago, but also more complicated, richer, sometimes simpler, and especially stranger than I had tried to depict it then—this was perhaps my strongest reason for rewriting the book.

MARGUERITE YOURCENAR

Mount Desert Island, 1959

Coup de Grâce
Marguerite Yourcenar

'One of the most imaginatively challenging novelists of the century'
PAUL BINDING, THE LITERARY REVIEW

Set in the Baltic provinces in the aftermath of World War I, *Coup de Grâce* tells the story of a strange and unhappy threesome: Erick, a young Prussian engaged with the White Russians in fighting the Bolsheviks; Conrad, the beloved friend of his youth; and Conrad's sister Sophie, whose unrequited love for Erick becomes an unbearable burden. An anguished intimacy grows up among the three young people, hemmed in by the civil war, fearful of the future and their own confused emotions.

'By grip and style and form, she is a major illuminator who is always a pleasure to read'
GEOFFREY GRIGSON, COUNTRY LIFE

'The book is one of those performances which, in its persistent artistry, its high concentration on sense impression and reflection, makes the strongest argument for the short novel form'
NEWSWEEK

'Told with great economy and restraint. It also has the sense of inevitability that so often marks works of exceptional quality'
MARTYN GOFF, DAILY TELEGRAPH

'Extraordinarily profound . . . The title is dreadfully precise'
GAY FIRTH, THE TIMES

0 552 99121 X   £2.50

BLACK SWAN

The Proprietor
Ann Schlee

'Rare and strange . . . rich in detail and steeped in the author's
sense of the period and place about which she writes, it
establishes Ann Schlee as one of the best new novelists we
have'
SUSAN HILL

The islands lay low and dark in the sea that had claimed the
lives of Adela Traherne's parents. Known to the islanders as
the Island Child, her life became inextricably linked with
Augustus Walmer, the Proprietor, in the summer of 1840 when
a group of his friends came to see how he was restoring the
economy and well-being of his people and the untamed beauty
of the islands he owned. None of the people who came
together in that summer was ever to forget what happened
then, none of them was ever to break free from the island's
grip, and the destinies of Adela and Augustus seemed fated to
be forever linked.

'Ambitious, imaginative . . . *The Proprietor* more than a little
resembles *The French Lieutenant's Woman*, with a dash of
Jamaica Inn, and an occasional nod in the direction of *The
Waves*'
ANITA BROOKNER, HARPERS & QUEEN

'Outstanding success . . . elegant precision and feeling for
period . . . attractive echoes of Charlotte Brontë and Elizabeth
Bowen'
HERMIONE LEE, THE OBSERVER

0 552 99099 X   £2.95

BLACK SWAN